Gayly

Complicated

www.BarbarianSpy.com

BarbarianSpy
Jindalee St
Toronto, 2283 NSW
Australia

Gayly

Complicated

A Collection of Gay Love Stories

by

shabbu

Table of Contents

PREFACE   7

CIRCUS MAXIMUS   9

MOVING ON   23

COMING FOR THE HONEY MAN   39

LYING INTO THE FUTURE   47

CAPTAIN'S OBSESSION   57

MISUNDERSTANDINGS   65

MATRYOSHKA KIDNAPPING   77

TWO CHANCES   91

HOOKUP GAMES   107

TURTLE AIRWAYS   113

ABOUT THE AUTHORS   127

Preface

Could anything ever be more complicated for a gay man? Nothing is as complicated as attempting an ongoing sexual relationship of one man with another. The uncertainties and suspicions and jealousies and misunderstandings that arise daily are legion. The difficulty in committing, accepting, and remaining constant, in an environment that cannot, as yet, find legal foundation almost anywhere, are presented for the reader, sometimes in frustrating, ships-passing-in-the-night fashion and more times than not in bittersweet sadness for opportunities lost, intentions misunderstood, loyalty sorely tested.

But there also are stories of love redeemed and commitment made and honored, and it is this sense of justification and "rightness" that the authors hope the reader will take away from this anthology—the knowledge of the possibility of sustained trust and deep understanding that the authors have found in each other in their merging into Shabbu to bring you literature made to combine sexual heat and thought-provoking prose.

Circus Maximus

Klaus

The next few seconds were crucial. I had to lock on Victor's wrists at exactly the right instant as he came out of his backward flip off the bar. If I missed, he would hit the hard wooden stage below us. We never used a net; men like us went through life without a safety net—only the strength and reliability of each other. And right at this instant, trembling as I never had before, I couldn't promise Victor strength, and I no longer believed in his reliability. In this business of split-second timing and regimentation, reliability was premier.

Victor had taken me in as a teenager when I had run away from home in Berlin when circuses were all the rage of Europe. He had trained me and nurtured me and protected me in the dangerous undercurrents that were circus life. And then when I had come of age, he had seduced me and shown me the ways of man loving man. He had glided the long, elegant fingers of his strong hands down my belly and beneath my balls and had entreated me in a low, hoarse voice to give him entrance, permission to both take and give pleasure. And trusting and loving him deeply, I had spread my legs for him, endured the initial pain and uncertainty, and then begged him not to stop as

9

those fingers found and parted my virginal bud and stretched and moistened me for the full, sobbing possession of his commanding manhood.

Circuses went out of style in Europe about the same time the Soviet empire was shattering and the European Union was, at last, taking meaningful shape. The thrill of uncertainly in Europe was dissipating. People wanted more subtle and sophisticated thrills in their lives, it seemed. Victor had to start reducing the number of trapeze artists in his troupe. The women went first, and then Serge and Fritz. Nothing told me that Victor loved me more than that he had let them go and not me. They were fully professional. My talents were more pronounced in his bed.

Just when I thought he would have to fold the act altogether, he discovered that the tastes in death-defying high trapeze acts were not dead in Europe; they had only become specialized, more sophisticated, more erotic. And there were opportunities that suited Victor and me exactly. There were private venues—special couples and men's clubs and gyms—in the underbelly of Europe—all over Europe—that welcomed specialized circus acts and were willing to pay well for them.

Thus was born the Circus Maximus, a very private circus act for very special venues.

There were always four of us in the act. But at first Victor tried an act with him and me performing on the high trapezes above two young Indonesian girls, who became better acquainted with each other on the stage below as Victor and I performed ever-more daring and dangerous flips and catches on the trapezes overhead. When we were done on the trapezes, we slid down on silken ropes and, as our finale, each fully stripped and fucked one of the Indonesian girls to the delight of the audiences.

Victor was to find that the all-male venues far surpassed those of the more conventional hedonists in profit and availability, though, and he settled on an act using two men from China instead of the Indonesian girls. And Victor found this more to his liking too. Teng was a monster of a muscle man and Ming was diminutive in comparison—still handsome and well formed, but not more than half the size of his counterpart.

Now while the scantily clad Victor and I flew overhead, Teng harried Ming below us, almost, but not quite to the point of penetration. When Victor and I descended on the silken cords in the new form of the act, Victor hung the diminutive Ming up on one of the trapeze poles by silken bonds on his wrists and Teng did the same with me on another pole, and Victor fucked Ming from the rear and Teng took me in mirrored form to the audience's moaning satisfaction.

The current act then ended with Victor and me climbing the silken cords again, doing one more death-defying pass on the trapeze, and winding up on one of the trapeze platforms with me doing a handstand, my body draped up Victor's, and Victor fucking down into me to a final burst of lights at the point of an ejaculation that wasn't always feigned.

Thus far the small, picky, well-heeled audiences had loved the act. And whereas Teng was as cruel with me each time as he was with Ming, Victor had claimed that Ming didn't interest him and that his sex with the small Chinese performer was feigned, only for show. And I had believed him—and trusted him—and had been rock solid in my catches of him high over the stage even though he was the heavier of we two by far and even when sometimes I felt he would pull my arms out of their sockets when hand didn't meet forearm precisely. But there had been no question I would be there for him, my protector and lover. No question. Until now.

The next to most difficult pass was this forward flip. It was happening now. I must not think about what I saw. I must make this catch.

Victor had said his fucking of Ming was only an act, that it meant nothing to him, and that, in contrast to what Teng did to me in each performance, Victor wasn't really even penetrating Ming in the act. Just faking it to a removed audience whose eyes were blinded by the stage lights and saw what they wanted to see. But he certainly was penetrating Ming when I saw them in Victor's dressing room the previous evening.

There had been a daybed in the dressing room, and I had arrived at the theater hours before Victor had expected me. I had said I needed a new pair of the ballet slippers we used in our high flying act and would have to go across Zurich—we were performing in Zurich's Aaah-Club in the Marktgasse—that afternoon to pick them up. But then I had found I already had another new pair and called and asked the shop to send the pair they had on to our next venue, at the Boléro on the Wollestraat in Bruges' Garenmarkt district, and I thus appeared at the theater much before Victor expected me.

I don't know if Victor would have been able to change appearances if I had knocked on the dressing room door—his cock was fully encased in the ass of the naked Ming, and they were both breathing heavily with heaving chests at the exertion of the fuck—but it had been years since I had knocked on Victor's door. There were no secrets between us. Or at least I had thought there were none. Before last night.

Neither of them had noticed me at first. Victor, fully naked, was kneeling on the daybed, his ass cheeks bouncing up and down on the heels of his feet. The small Chinese youth was on his back facing Victor, his thighs pulled up over Victor's hips and his butt mounds sliding along Victor's thighs, as Victor, with strong hands holding the small man's waist, pulled Ming back and forth on his prodigious, hard, skewering dick.

Not long after I found them, and while I was still too much in shock to say or do anything, Ming cried out in passion and spouted his cream up Victor's belly—and Victor, in turn, groaned and jerked, and spent himself inside the Chinese youth's channel. There was nothing the least bit feigned about this sex act.

Victor was turned away from me, but Ming saw me when freed of the throes of passion, and the satisfied, sly look he gave me spoke volumes.

I turned and fled the room, not knowing if Ming told Victor what I'd seen.

That night was just a "spot" run through of the act on the Aaah-Club stage, making sure the equipment was set up correctly and the distances were proper—nothing is more important in the high trapeze world than that the distances between everything are properly measured. Victor didn't seem to notice that I was particularly quiet and pale or that Ming went out of his way to stand in my spotlights and to be bitchy—until Teng dragged him off into the wings and fucked him silly on a stack of backdrop curtains to the cries of pain and indignation from the possibly newly empowered Ming.

Tonight was the first real performance in Zurich since I saw Victor fucking Ming. Tonight we would know how hard reliability could be tested. I knew I didn't want Victor to fall. But I couldn't be sure that what I told myself I "knew" was what I really "knew." And I felt sick to my stomach, and all atremble, and weak in my muscles as we set up and tested the bars for our swing out and fastened our eyes on each other's to gauge the exact moment of our takeoff, off over the bare, wooden stage.

At the last split second, Victor's eyes showed astonishment and fear and a deep questioning—caused I'm sure by whatever he saw in my eyes in that instant. But it was too late to check; we both had already leaned out over the platforms into our bars far too much not to swing out. As I swung out, I experienced contrasting, warring feelings that I never had felt before.

* * * *

Victor

At the last split second, I knew. I knew that Klaus was different tonight. The way he looked at me. What was wrong? I had no idea. And I was afraid, as I had never been before with him.

Fear is the most dangerous thing in an act like ours. The fear of not being caught by your partner, of falling. It's that which makes you fall. That I also knew, and I tried to crush it, to let go of everything but my faith in Klaus, in his professionalism, if nothing else.

"No. No. Think of nothing except what I must do and do it right. Klaus will be there. Klaus will be there. Klaus will be there to catch me," I repeated to myself as I swung out.

I executed my backward flip perfectly and Klaus caught me. A good firm catch. As he should, as he should. All is well in that way at least. Now turn, and run my feet and legs up between his arms and slide down. Now, there, yes, his arms wrapped firmly about my legs as I hang upside down and reach up, stroke my cock through the padded fabric of my tiny costume, the padding making my package look massive and my cock hard. Yes, the audience loves that. He has me firmly.

But why? Why the look? Oh . . . no don't think of that, just stroke and smile and get ready—count, count, to swing off and catch my own bar again. We have done this so many times, so many times.

3 . . . 2 . . . 1 . . .

I remember when I first saw Klaus hanging around the tent of the circus my act was performing with at the time, and looking lost and brash all at once. Too young to be living on the streets, I had thought, and I had wanted to save him from that. And I took him in—he said he wanted to be in the circus, and he was lithe and light, easy to use in the act.

He had no great talent but tried hard and learned well enough. In the beginning he was so lean and light we tossed him back and forth between us, Serge, Fritz, and me, even the girl, Ludmilla, had caught him and thrown him back to me when he first joined us.

Then he had grown up and grown to be a wild, lean young man of great beauty. I was suddenly in love with him, for his youth and beauty. And when he was grown he had responded to me as no man ever had since Franz. Franz who had gone to America to train and teach gymnastics while I had accepted I would never be internationally competitive and remained in Germany and moved on to the trapeze and circus life.

But now Klaus has grown into a well-filled man, not tall and broad of muscle like me, but also not longer small and lithe. And sometimes I have a passionate lusting for lithe, small bodies. To fuck men who seem delicate and fragile as they moan and twist beneath me. That is my secret fetish. Klaus is still shorter than me and leaner, but not as he once was; he is the man I want in my life. But sex and heat, ahhh, sometimes what I feel in my cock and balls when some lithe and slender young man is available. Ahhh.

Ming. Now Ming is all that one could want in litheness and small size. Yes, at first I had not fucked him properly upon the stage, but feeling his small, seemingly defenseless body under me night after night, I had finally been desperate to have him.

But I controlled myself, for I knew Klaus had never been with another man except for when our act required it. But Ming was so desirable. So desirable . . .

Ming. Ming. I do not really like to hear the way Teng takes Klaus, but it is a good act and Klaus does not complain.

In fact, Ming says that Klaus likes what Teng does—that he sometimes likes it rough and hard. I am not sure if what he ways is true. I don't think so. I think Ming makes it up.

One day when Klaus was out, Ming came to me in my dressing room to ask why I didn't fuck him properly on stage, and he cried and said, "If you do not find me attractive enough, Victor, then there was no place for me in your show."

He was wearing only a pair of tight stretch shorts, and I could see his cock lying under the fabric and growing as he talked to me, and I could plainly see the longing way he looked at me.

He has a fine almost androgynous body. And he looked at me with big, wide tear-filled eyes and said, "I look at you and you are so handsome and strong, I long for you to fuck me, to feel your big cock in my ass. But . . . but you cannot even do it as part of your act."

He was most upset, but at the same time aroused, and seeing his erection growing in his tight shorts, I was getting hard myself, for he is very desirable.

"Perhaps if we practice here in private you can find a way to fuck me properly in spite of your dislike; then I will not feel humiliated in front of the audience," he said to me with his lips trembling, and he fell to his knees and began to suck on my pole through the light fabric of my shorts for all I was wearing was boxers as I was relaxing.

"Of course I would like to fuck you properly," I said honestly, the feel of his mouth on me so good, but I tried to push him away.

"But—" I did not know how to say it, and his mouth, ahhhh, " . . . but Klaus is my partner; we are like man and wife, and he may not like it that I am enjoying fucking another man every day."

Ming looked up at me, his hand rubbing my engorged rod, "Ahh, but your Klaus, he is writhing under Teng each day.

He moans for Teng to plow him roughly. I have heard him, Victor," Ming told me, his bottom lip trembling again. "But you cannot even fuck me properly in the show; the audience knows, and they will wonder why you find me so ugly. Or they will wonder if I am sick, if I have some disease, which you know is not true."

He was crying now even as he pulled my cock free of my shorts and swallowed the head of it. I pulled him up then. I was aroused by him and ready to fuck, but I tried to reassure and comfort him.

I hugged him, and he pressed his hard rod to my thigh, and his hand found its way to my hard cock and, well, and in a short time, my rod was standing out and he had his shorts down around his ankles and was bending over the daybed in the dressing room and spreading his checks for me and begging me, "Victor, please, I want to feel you inside me. Show me that you do not find me ugly and can really fuck me. Please Victor."

And as I really did want Ming, my cock quickly found its way to his hole, and I worked it in, eagerly. Here was the perfect answer to my fetish. A fetish for small and slender young men just like Ming, which I have always occasionally had to satisfy.

Ahh, and once I had fucked his tight but experienced channel once, it was too tempting when I was able to do it again. And I began to fuck him properly in the act. Then yesterday he came to the dressing room while Klaus was away shopping and I wasn't able to stop myself from plowing him energetically again. Him lying back on the daybed with his legs about my hips, me fucking into him long and hard. His small smooth body under me moaning, writhing. Ahhhh.

Now I turn over and Klaus grips my wrists and I swing up and he lets go.

Catch. Yes, I have my bar now, ready to swing up to the plate again and stop while Klaus swings up and joins me.

"What is wrong?" I hiss at him as he lands beside me.

"Ming," Klaus replies.

"Ming? Ming has nothing to do with us."

"You are fucking Ming and you say he has nothing to do with us?"

I have no idea how Klaus has discovered that I have fucked Ming. And I am horrified that he knows. There have been others, not many, but yes, others. My fetish overwhelms me at times and must be satisfied. But I had thought he did not even suspect them, they have nothing to do with how I feel about him and us. How did he discover?

"You are the one I live with as if we were married Klaus."

"For how much longer. How long will it take Ming to take my place?"

"He can never take your place," I said adamantly. "You are worrying about nothing. Nothing important has happened. I fuck him for the show, the audience could tell I was not doing it properly," I said, "He—"

But Klaus swung off angrily before I could say more, and what more could I say. I love him and he must know that, but now I have no idea if I can trust him to catch me.

Ming. I would not want him up here where I have to rely on him. No, I may have fucked him but I do not trust him. And I do not believe what he says about Teng and Klaus.

Klaus, Klaus. I cannot manage without him. And the act, the act needs two men who can connect properly as we do. This is a good act. And I love him. I cannot lose him.

There Ming is, down there with that Teng. I do not like Teng, and he mistreats Ming. But why then, why does Ming not leave him?

* * * *

Ming

Teng was harassing me more than usual, and I was more than fed up with it. If he did not know my secret, I would have gone off months before. But he knew and he was nasty and violent and twice my size. But Victor will soon want me more than Klaus, and Victor is German, he can stand up to Teng and send him away.

Yes, Victor would do that for me in a few days I knew. "Hah," I thought, as Teng grabbed me yet again and forced me to my knees before him. "You will not be bothering me and using me like your private plaything for much longer, you pig."

I bit down hard on his fat cock as he stuffed it into my mouth and he let out a cry of pain.

"I will tell. I well tell the police," Teng is hissing at me in Cantonese as he lays me back and lifts my legs. He is supposed to pretend he wants to fuck me and I keep rolling away, but I am afraid as he has been drinking tonight. His fingers are digging in to me and my cries are not made up. He is really hurting me tonight.

"Pig," I hiss at him, "Pig."

"Cheat, liar," he hisses back. "What if I tell your good friend Victor that you are an illegal immigrant and wanted by the police already? Hah. Will he put you up on the trapeze with him then?"

I lie there hating him, and he does what he is not supposed too; he smiles at me and laughs as he begins to push his fingers into me hard.

"I hate you," I yelp and hiss at him.

I look up to the heights of the stage for relief. Victor will be coming down the silken rope at any moment; Teng is not supposed to fuck me in the act; Victor is. I'm not sure Teng will hold back tonight, though. I must hold him off, though. Let him unleash his lust on Klaus instead. Yes, and leave Victor to me.

* * * *

Just Hold On

The pass high above the stage of Zurich's Aaah-Club had been executed perfectly, but both Victor and Klaus knew this wasn't just a typical act night. They both could feel the tension—and, worse, the indecision—in the other during the catch. But the catch had held, perfectly. They were swinging back to their own platforms and both pirouetted, almost in unison—only someone who had watched the act a million times would have known the maneuver wasn't perfect—and turned and stood on their respective platforms, their chalk-covered swing bars held in one hand and the other one lifted, acknowledging the clapping and raucous cheers from the drunken men in the audience below, most of whom were actually watching the performance rather than engaged in a performance of their own on their neighbor in the shadowed banquettes.

Victor looked into Klaus's eyes across the strobe-lit stage. Snapping into the routine of gaining eye contact, both started another numbered cadence, forming the numbers with their lips so they would be in synch and could time their next—and most difficult—swing out perfectly. Klaus was there, as always, ready, as always. But not as always, there were tears in his eyes.

Why, Victor thought. Why did these relationships with other men have to be so complicated? Why couldn't men just enjoy each other's bodies, fuck who and when they pleased and just enjoy each other's company? What was so important about constancy or commitment in the world of men fucking men?

Victor began the count: 7 . . . 6. His eyes glanced down at the performers below. Teng had Ming in a torso hold, with Ming facing the back of the stage. Teng was fucking Ming with the bulbous fingers of one hand, letting the audience see that the penetration was genuine. But Ming was looking up, straight up, at Klaus. And the hatred Victor saw in Ming's eyes, made Victor flinch.

4 . . . 3 . . .

It was that flinch that did it. Victor swung out on 3, as by instinct. He was to swing on 3 so that when Klaus swung out on 1, Victor would have had time to leave his bar at the apex of its swing, do a back flip, and be around in position to meet Klaus.

But with the split second it took to register Ming's glare at Klaus, Victor's 3 was Klaus's 2.

It was a miracle that Klaus even caught both of Victor's hands in his, let alone managed a firmer, surer hold up farther on the forearms, allowing the hands of both a more steady grip. It could have been called merely a fingertip grip, putting all of the centrifugal weight of Victor on the fingers of the hands. Even the stronger Serge or Fritz would not have been able to hold this grip. With the smaller, weaker Klaus, the grip should have been impossible, and Victor should have crashed to the wooden stage below.

But Klaus did maintain his grip as they swung, first back toward Klaus's platform and then out again to where Victor's bar was swinging back to them.

It seemed like forever, as Victor's panic-filled eyes locked on Klaus's tear-filled eyes, backdropped by the gasps and clapping and cries of approval from the unknowing audience. Victor saw much more than tears, though—or even the strain of fighting the slippery grip of sweaty fingers or the horrific strain of Victor's weight on Klaus's shoulder sockets. He saw determination and constancy and commitment, and, above all love.

And then Victor had released and caught his bar and they were both on their own platforms. To the audience, this was nothing more than a well-performed, dangerous, very sexy circus act successfully delivered. To Victor, however, the whole world had changed. His whole perspective had changed.

This was where Klaus and Victor were supposed to slide down the silken ropes to the stage, simultaneously, to move on to the next phase of the act with Teng and Ming. But when Klaus looked over to Victor's platform to start the descent, he was surprised to see that Victor wasn't there. Victor already was gliding down the silken rope to the stage below.

Klaus was mortified. Victor didn't trust him anymore, Klaus reasoned. Although they had managed the last back-flip swing out, he hadn't caught Victor solidly. It was over. Victor would replace him now, wouldn't ever trust him on the trapezes again.

Dejected, Klaus reached for his own silken rope down to the stage and slowly descended, completely defeated. Well, not completely defeated, he briefly mused. He couldn't be replaced with Ming. At least there was that. Ming was far too small to swing in the heavens with Victor.

When Klaus reached the stage, it was deserted. The act had completely fallen apart. This was where Victor was supposed to bind Ming and suspend him by raised arms from hooks on his platform pole and simulate a fuck of him, while Teng was supposed to do the same with Klaus on Klaus's platform pole. But no one was there when Klaus reached the stage. That was only a momentary absence, though. Just as Klaus was wondering what he should do to cover up the disintegration of the act, Victor reappeared, pulling a small velvet-covered platform from the back stage center, a platform that was used in another of the club's sex acts.

When Victor had reached the stage himself, he had parted the surprised Teng and Ming and motioned them off stage, Teng to stage left and Ming to stage right. He would take care of both Teng and Ming, but that would have to be later. Teng was too brutal and Ming was a trouble-making minx. They would probably both have to go from the act, but for now he owed Ming at least the protection of sending them to different sides of the stage wings where Teng couldn't get to Ming—and Ming couldn't do any more damage in Victor's relationship with Klaus.

When Victor had returned and centered the small, velvet-covered platform, he moved over to a surprised Klaus and theatrically—because they were, after all, in the middle of a performance for an audience of raunchy men—stripped Klaus of his tight, silk pants and his jock, rendering him naked except for the sequined sweat bands on his wrists and the matching choker at his neck. Then Victor similarly stripped himself.

Victor gently lay Klaus on his back on the velvet platform, spread and lifted his legs, and made long, languid, deeply penetrating love to his young companion. Putting on one hell of a sex performance for the audience of the Aaah-Club, a convincing master fucking that was talked about in the club for weeks to come. But, much more important, showing Klaus how deeply and intensely Victor loved him and how much better he now understood the power and importance of constancy and commitment.

Moving On

Terry

I had finally returned to the grounds of Oakton Park to scatter Luke's ashes.

We had spent the last two months of Luke's life in a small cottage in the grounds of the main house, and it had been Luke's wish that the grounds should be the final resting place for his ashes. I had wanted them to go somewhere that I could return to to mourn him. But in those last weeks, he had been insistent. And I couldn't break the promise he had forced me to make to him.

The main house at Oakton Park was the English home of a distant cousin of Luke's, and an elderly aunt arranged with its owner for us to have the use of the cottage while Luke was still well enough to remain at home—because, unfortunately, we didn't have a home of our own to spend that time in.

We had spent our lives moving around the globe, going from one promising mineral exploration project to another. Luke had begun his career in the high, dry mountains of South America before moving on to the jungles of Indonesia and Borneo. I had begun mine in the Australian desert, before I met Luke on my first job in Kalimantan. There had been an instant affinity between us, but we had tried to ignore the physical attraction. He was the site manager and senior geologist, and I was one of several geo's working directly under him. The harmony and smooth operation of a remote mining camp can be upset by a lot of things. And any sexual relationship on site would have been almost impossible to keep secret.

It had finally happened one night when we had both had to fly to Kuala Lumpur for different reasons. Me to go on to Jakarta for a job interview. Luke to go for the monthly management meeting in KL.

There had been a mix-up with the company's bookings, and the hotel had a conference group filling every spare room. We had wound up saying we'd share the one room they had reserved for MM Mining and Exploration.

We both knew why I was going to Jakarta, and the knowledge we might only see each other for a few weeks more and might never meet again had us both anxious and relieved at the same time. We shared dinner and a few drinks, and it turned out that both of us were thinking the same thing all through the meal. The conference crowd were noisy and wanting to party, and neither of us was interested in the noise and carry on, so we headed back to our room early. Both having early flights was a good excuse.

Luke's hand brushed my ass in the lift, and my cock twitched at the touch. I was instantly in heat for him. And it must have shown in my face, as he moved closer, and by the time the lift reached the eleventh floor, he had his hand on my package and was kissing my neck from behind, as I reached back to pull his head closer to mine and pressed his hand harder against my engorging dick. His drill was already resting hard and incredibly long against the crease of my ass cheeks.

It was several months since I had left the jungle camp last and had let myself be in heat. I also felt as if I had known Luke all my life and might never see him again, and I knew that there could be no problems about anything that happened between us that night. We both knew that the interview I was going to was almost a formality. In a few weeks I'd be gone.

So we both let go. Completely. I was already unbuttoning my shirt as we entered our room, and Luke closed the door and came up to me, and we kissed hungrily as he ran his hands up and down my torso while I removed my shirt. Then his hands followed down to run inside my briefs as I undid my pants, his hands pushing them down as I wrapped my arms about him, and we kissed. Both of us were moaning, and I was whimpering with need. His strong hands squeezed my dick and balls, then moved to my butt cheeks and massaged them as he devoured my mouth. And I had trouble pulling free of his embrace to drop to my knees before him and unzip his pants and pull his throbbing tool free.

I sank my mouth over his cap and ran my tongue in and around his dripping slit, catching the precum leaking from him. He pulled my head in to him, and his nine-inch tool sank into my throat. But was way too much for me to take, so I wrapped one hand around the root of it and worked my mouth hungrily over the rest. But Luke quickly pulled free and took hold of my arms; pulling me up and tossing me back onto the bed. He loomed over me, and I spread and lifted my thighs as I grabbed his hands and pulled him to me.

"Never without protection," he'd growled and lurched free.

I stroked myself as I watched his muscular but lean body as he emptied his bag on the floor, hunting for a condom. In a moment he was back, and I tore open the packet with trembling hands as he lifted my hips and dropped his mouth to my exposed entrance. Then I was rolling the latex on him and he was roughly fingering my ass. We were both in a rush. We'd waited too long and were too much in heat for each other to go slowly.

I cried out in pain as he entered me, but once he had sunk to the limit inside me, I wanted everything he was giving me. I was moaning and yelping as he moved his cock inside me, wanting more, and he was moaning and grunting as he dug deep and plowed me hard.

I got the job, but a month later Luke joined me. He'd pulled strings and was made site manager, and right from the start it wasn't a secret that we shared the same cabin.

We'd had ten good years. Then Luke had become ill, and we had done the rounds of half a dozen specialists before he was diagnosed, and by then it was too late. After consulting with the doctors, Luke told me he had contracted a nasty strain of malaria when he first went to Borneo years before, but had managed it. He always worked hard and caught some fever in Kalimantan that he tried to ignore. Unfortunately, it hadn't gone away, and with the malaria it had been too much.

So we'd come to Oakton Park and had walked in the grounds on his good days and sat together, talking in a sheltered spot in the sun on his bad ones. And we had made gently careful love on occasion. He insisted on using pills so we could, and I didn't stop him, wanting that bond, though it tired him. Then one day he insisted I go to London to get him a book he really wanted to read. I didn't want to leave him.

His distant cousin, the one who owned Oakton Place, was Hugh B. Caul, the famous thriller writer. I had an idea he had left a wife somewhere in the states and now seemed to be spending most of his time at Oakton Place. When we were there, he had a couple of good-looking young research assistants staying at the house. Both were male. And one night when we were making love Luke told me that Hugh had been his first. Hugh had been twenty-three and Luke had been eighteen. It had been summer, and they had spent it holidaying together on the east coast of the Chesapeake Bay, on the Maryland coast n the States, staying at old inns and guest houses in the quaint waterside villages.

At the cottage Hugh would drop in on us to sit and reminisce with Luke. At first they didn't seem very alike, but, as they interacted, they more and more resembled each other. And, eventually, seeing Hugh full of health and vitality next to a frail, thin Luke, I saw what Luke could have been like in a few more years, if he had remained healthy. I saw a graying but handsome man, tall, straight, and well muscled and athletic still at forty-eight. And I always had to leave them, and go outside alone to wait, until I was needed or Hugh left.

* * * *

Hugh

I had acceded to Luke's request to settle in at Oakton Park. I never even considered telling him no. It wasn't just that I felt guilty—that I was responsible for having brought this on—but after all these years, I still loved him. He had intrigued and attracted me all through our childhood, even though our "separated by the pond" families only gathered every couple of years.

Luke's family had been going down as mine was rising. Finally, to save the ancestral home at Oakton Park, my family had been forced to buy the place, and that's when we started coming to England every summer.

Luke was always somewhat of a recluse, and there was only me there in the summer anywhere close to his age, even though I was five years his senior. He followed me around like a puppy dog. I had wanted him since I was nineteen, but I managed to hold off until he was eighteen.

And then I took him. It was selfish and cruel of me, but at least I held off until he was old enough to make his own decision. And he worshiped me enough that there was no question about giving himself to me. But not in England. I actually planned it in advance. That is what I was most ashamed of—that I'd schemed to have him, to change his life forever, to put him on the path to where he ended up.

I had to have him alone, away from his element, away from both his family and mine. I suggested that he celebrate his eighteenth birthday with his first trip to the States, which I paid for. I took him to the Maryland eastern shore of the Chesapeake, and we roamed the old harbor towns of Rock Hall, Chestertown, St. Michael's, and, finally, Oxford, where I made my move. We were both good sailors. I took him out on the Tred Avon and then into the bay, where we dropped the anchor, brought the sails in, and I fucked him three ways from Sunday on the teak roof of the yacht's cabin. He wanted me as much as I wanted him. I didn't have to ask or to do more than lay a hand on his sweet ass, and then he was laying back, pulling me with him, spreading his legs wide and writhing under me in ecstasy.

I had opened a Pandora's box. After that Luke couldn't get enough. And it wasn't just me. He quickly moved on to others, and he traded himself indiscriminately. I tried to make him stop or to at least be more careful. But he wouldn't listen to me, and we parted on bad terms. We didn't speak again until he asked to move back to Oakton Park. But I heard about him. Other members of the family had seen us move toward each other, and they weren't dummies. They knew what I had done, and they made sure over the years that I heard how active and indiscriminate Luke had been. They wanted to punish me. And I can't say that I blamed them for that.

Then I heard that he had met "the one" and had calmed down. I don't know if he stopped sleeping around then, but a cousin visited him and subsequently let me know that at least he was being safe now.

But I wasn't surprised when he finally called me, seeking sanctuary for his final journey. I wasn't surprised that he had waited too long.

I felt responsible. I felt guilty. I could do my writing anywhere; my own young men could easily move with me; I had employed them to keep them close at hand, for it to be convenient for them to share my bed, often both of them together. I was as weak as Luke was. I'm not sure, but it may have been a family trait. But I was more careful than Luke had been.

So when Luke and his Terry moved into the cottage at Oakton Park, I returned to the main house as well. There wasn't much I could do for him now other than to be nearby and to ensure that he received the best of care. Other than his name and that my cousin had said that he was steadying influence on Luke, I hadn't known this Terry guy at all before they had come to Oakton Park. And, considering the situation, I had to accept that he might bail out on Luke at any moment. Someone had to be there, and I felt guilty enough to take that responsibility.

On the afternoon of the day Luke died, I saw Terry drive off in their car. I'm ashamed to say that my first thought was that this was the day he was bailing out. I only saw him leave because I was taking one of my assistants up against the window enclosure of my library in the main house, as I often did when I was tense about a needed change of direction in one of my manuscripts. As soon as I finished with him, though, I cleaned up and walked over to the cottage.

I found Luke, frail and washed out, lying on a sofa in the cottage's parlor.

"No, he hasn't left me," Luke said with some difficulty. "I sent him away. To London. But he should only be gone for the day. I told him I needed a book. I had difficulty deciding on a book that he couldn't produce from the house library."

"Is he getting on your nerves then?" I asked, half hoping that this was the case. Terry was entirely too good and noble for me not to like him. And I really was desperate not to like him. In the back of my mind, I still wanted Luke for myself.

"No, Terry's a brick. Always has been," Luke responded with a sigh. Not exactly what I wanted to hear. "I just needed him not to be here today."

And then to my next question, he responded. "No, Terry doesn't know the whole of it. He thinks I have a rare form of malaria. That's what I told him the doctors told me. He doesn't know. But I've been careful with Terry. There won't be any problem with Terry. We've been together for more than ten years, and there's been no problem for Terry."

"He should know, Luke. He should be told. He has the right to know."

"But he'll leave me," Luke said with a low whine. "He'll leave me then."

"Maybe, Luke," I said. "But he still has a right to know. And I'll be here even if he leaves. But if you don't tell him, I will."

"I feel so cold," Luke said. "Then it really has come to that. Come hold me, Hugh. Hold me close."

I went to him and held him close in my arms and rocked him gently back and forth.

"Fuck me, Hugh," Luke murmured. "Let me feel you inside me one last time."

"I'm sorry," Luke, I said. "You aren't strong enough for that. That's no longer possible."

"Make love to me . . . please. I'm so afraid." Luke was quietly crying now.

So, I did what little I could. I unzipped his pants and pulled out his cock and stroked him endlessly until he managed to find release.

"I need my pills, Hugh," he whispered. "In the cabinet over the kitchen sink. A full bottle. I need that."

"There's a full bottle here on the floor, Luke," I said. "It must have fallen off the table. You have enough medicine right here."

Luke sighed and turned his face to the sofa, and that was that. He didn't speak to me again, and he closed his eyes. After it seemed that his breathing had become as regular as his disease would permit, I rose from the sofa, lowering his head from my lap to the pillow, and quietly went over to a wingback chair by the hearth and sat and watched the sleeping figure. I was concerned for Luke, but I also had deadlines on the proofs of my current book. I didn't see the harm of slipping up to the main house and bringing those back so I could continue to work while he slept.

I hadn't gotten more than half way back to the main house when I heard the dreaded sound. I have no idea how he'd managed to get the gun. My first thought was a profound regret that I hadn't just given him that second bottle of pills.

* * * *

Terry

When Luke insisted I go to London, I didn't want to leave, but he assured me that Hugh had visited earlier while I was in the garden and had agreed to sit with him while I was away. So I went. I had no choice. He sent me away. But if I'd had any notion why, I wouldn't have left. Even after Hugh had told me what Luke really had been sick from.

For a long time after he died, I hated Luke for what he had done to me. Not that he had not told me what really was wrong with him, but that he hadn't had faith that I would stay with him regardless. And I hated Hugh too, for making it easy for him to go as he did.

And as soon as I had Luke's ashes, I left the country. I had got a job through contacts, and a week after his death I was back in the dry, dusty, red desert of Australia. For months I spent each night holding the urn containing Luke clutched to my chest. Telling him how unfair it was for him to leave me before I was ready. Then one night I was able to leave the urn containing his ashes in the bottom of my bag, and just hold them occasionally.

After twelve months, my contract was up, and I was free and ready to do what Luke had wanted me to, what he had told me in a message he'd left behind that I'd only found after leaving England with his urn.

So there I was, standing on the driveway of Oakton Place holding the urn containing all that remained of Luke and waiting for Hugh to join me.

* * * *

Hugh

Terry was standing there in the drive, apparently not sure whether he should go immediately to the cottage or come to the main house. I hated myself at that moment.

I hated myself because I wanted him. It had slowly crept up on me that I wanted him after the noble way he held himself after Luke died—not to mention how he had handled Luke's sickness. I wanted him because he was sweet and all that another would want in a partner as a helpmate. But more than that I wanted him because he was one nice piece of ass. I could understand why Luke was willing to change his life for this man—even if he had done so too late. I could change my life for this man too, I thought.

At that moment, as I saw him standing, full of indecision and sadness, in the car park of Oakton Park, I told myself that I could leave off with my own form of promiscuity and settle down with this man. Not only because of how he lived his life, but also because he was achingly sexy. He could cure my urges just as he would have cured Luke's if he'd come along soon enough.

With a great sigh, I left my library window and went down to him. It turned out that he wasn't wondering where to go. He had a last request to perform for Luke, one that he

31

couldn't wait now to get beyond him. He told me that he couldn't move on with his life until he had done this for Luke. And Terry was waiting for me to come down and go out to the edge of the lake with him to consign Luke's ashes to the water. The very act of watching Luke's ashes drifting on the top of the water, ever so briefly before they sank below the surface, affected me deeply. I couldn't help but think back on that first time out on the waters of Chesapeake Bay, when Luke's fate was set into motion—by me, by my weakness and greed.

When we came back up the lawn from the lake, I instinctively turned toward the cottage when Terry did, although we hadn't spoken more than a couple of words with each other, and that had been on the drive when he told me what he had to do with the ashes.

Tears were streaming down Terry's face when we entered the cottage, and I just guided him back to the bedroom and we sat there together on the edge of the bed. At first it was just a comradely hug, a shared grieving for the tragedy of Luke's life. But, without realizing it, I found myself trying to kiss away the tears in Terry's eyes. And then he lifted his face toward me. I could see that he seemed to be in a daze. I could have guessed why it happened as it did.

When he looked into my eyes, his face seemed to brighten, and he gave me a dazzling smile. Then we couldn't get enough of each other. We were hugging and kissing and tearing at each other's clothes. He was arched back on the bed, and I was kissing his nipples and working my way down across his stomach and possessing his manhood with my mouth.

Terry was on his belly on the bed, his hands grasping the rods of the headboard and his rounded butt cheeks rising off the bed, offering themselves to me, when I wedged his thighs between my knees and entered him strongly. We moaned and sighed in harmony as we fucked in a rhythm that seemed so natural, that seemed like we had done this for years. And we rode on and on, me trawling deeper, holding longer, pulling farther out and then digging deeper, as Terry cried out in ecstasy at the taking. He cried out for me again when I pulled half out of him and grasped the root of my cock and twisted it around inside him—just as Luke had cried out when I'd done this to him. So I continued doing it. I set a pattern to the fuck that was so familiar in my lovemaking with Luke that I was transported back to a happier time. I had no idea it was also familiar to Terry.

And then at the point of my ejaculation, Terry threw his head back and cried out in the deepest passion. "Oh, Yes! . . . Luke!"

I should have known. He was on pills. He'd told me he was—that he'd had to do so to get through this last ordeal with the consignment of Luke's ashes. I should have known that in his state he would mistake me for Luke.

* * * *

Terry

I felt that I had only let Hugh make love to me because he reminded me of Luke so much. In his appearance and his mannerisms, in small ways, like the way he lifted one eyebrow when he was listening to something Luke was saying. The way he twisted his cock inside my ass just like Luke. That had always driven me wild.

On the bed in the cottage, I had come myself almost immediately after Hugh had, with Luke's name still ringing in the bedroom, and my cream soaking into the sheet beneath me. And I had been fully connected to Luke. But as I fell back to the bed, exhausted and recovering myself, Luke's cock didn't remain buried up my ass; he didn't rub his chest against my back he way he always did; he didn't bring his mouth to my neck and kiss it.

Instead, I felt him pull away and slip out of me, and I had turned, whimpering for the expected continuation of his fuck. And, and . . . I had realized through the haze I was in that the man leaving the bed and standing on the cottage floor was not Luke. It was a moment before I understood the man who had fucked me so much like my dead lover did was Hugh, Luke's distant cousin. And he was now pale and grim and the facial resemblance to Luke was largely gone.

But then he smiled at me, and I saw Luke again.

"You can be so alike," I gasped in anguish.

And I buried my head in the pillow and cried some more, with Hugh sitting beside me and resting a hand on my shoulder.

"You can stay here for a couple of days," he said, "If you want to. As long as you like," he added, squeezing my shoulder.

"I'm sorry," I replied, "You are, you are just so like him at times."

My long-held bitterness at Hugh was gone. Now I felt thoughtless that I had let what had happened happen. That I had cried out to Luke as Hugh had flooded me with his seed. And I wondered why in his last message to me Luke had insisted that I could only release his ashes if Hugh was there with me. Perhaps he had foreseen this, perhaps he had understood that I might see him in Hugh. Maybe he had thought I would need someone to reawaken my desire. But he had been wrong, instead our lovemaking had left me feeling guilty and more alone.

But Hugh's hand on my body was like a brand, marking me, connecting me to a man I could physically desire but didn't know, and I cried again when he took it away and left me. And I wished that instead of leaving he had tied my wrists to the bed's fancy Victorian bed head with its curving and twining steel and had fucked me hard and made me cry out for him. Cry his name. Make me his.

But this wasn't real. No. I was sure my new desire for Hugh was only me trying to recapture what I had with Luke. That, and the pills I had taken to make the difficult parting from my last physical connection with Luke easy. To me his ashes had become him.

I was confused and desperate to escape and headed back to the Australian desert. Wanting to get the feel of both Luke and Hugh out of my mind. I felt I needed to move on with my life, not wallow in the absence of Luke any longer.

I had been working in the Tanami desert for eighteen months, moving around to different leases, doing initial sampling work, and now was back in the main camp for a few days in the office. After dinner on my first night, I went to the back of the canteen to check the mail and smiled at the postbag waiting for me.

"Have you heard?" Jack said, coming up behind me, "That writer, Hugh Caul, has been in an accident, a car crash in the Alps. He's been badly burned."

I was too shocked to feel anything, I could only say petulantly, "No. Where did you hear that? I don't believe it."

"Last night, on the BBC news. It's true. I just hope he's OK. I've been enjoying the books you've lent me. Wouldn't want him to have written his last one," he said, before hurrying off.

Back in my demountable I slit open the plastic postbag and pulled out *Dead Lover's Gift*, Hugh Caul's latest bestseller. I held it in my hands and looked at it. I wasn't sure why I had started to read his books in particular. I just did. With Luke there had been little time for anything but work and sex.

In ten years together we hadn't gradually had less sex, like most couples do. Luke's appetite had remained large, and I had developed a taste for frequent sex and only had to see him look at me to start getting an erection. And I had never hesitated to indulge any desire I might have for him. I generally took, but there were times I rode him equally hard, and I had come to expect us to share our bodies every night.

But since his death, I'd adjusted to celibacy on site and had filled my spare time with reading, and somehow I had started to read Hugh's books. Luke had been quiet and intense, introverted, but intensely sensual. At work he had been methodical and thorough, always serious. But the Hugh I had found lurking in his novels had a wicked sense of humor and a sharp eye for people's hypocrisies. He was a sophisticated urbane observer, a far cry from Luke's almost total preoccupation with his work as a geologist.

And now that I was no longer young and my career had reached a plateau I wasn't as content as I had been. I was alone on the lonely isolated sites where the work I knew best was, and I was starting to wonder if the world Luke and I had shared so contentedly was really mine now, without him.

I lay on the bed and clutched Hugh's book to myself, and my mind ran in a hundred directions, trying to get away for the news but always coming back to Hugh burned and perhaps dying. And I cried for him, for not being able to be with him at such a terrible time. And I cried too at the thought of losing him. But he'd let me go so easily that afternoon I had mistaken him for Luke. I was struggling with myself. I had tried moving on with my life; I had tried to bury the memory of Luke—and that short encounter with his cousin as well. But, whereas I could think of Luke with bittersweet appreciation mellowing memory now, I still could only think of Hugh with almost a visceral sexual heat that radiated through my body and had me seeking privacy and the relief of my stroking hand.

I tried to dispel the rising of arousal at the remembrance of that brief love making with Hugh by lying back on the bed and opening his latest book. I looked at the first page and read the title again: *Dead Lover's Gift.*

As I read, the voice of the book's narrator became that of Hugh, and the farther into the book I read, the more I realized that he had written the book to be about Hugh and me. The situation of Luke's last few months and his death were slightly changed in the book, but I, who had lived them, clearly discerned the underlying tragedies and truths in what he wrote. And what began to rise out of these written truths as I read on was Hugh's voice crying out to me. What I had seen as him so easily letting me go that day after we had made confused love after consigning Luke's ashes to the lake waters, was strongly belied here in his writings. His book described in deeply painful terms how hard it was for him to let go of the character who so obviously was me.

In a climatic sequence in the book, he wrote of coming upon my character, exhausted from the caring for and suicide of his lover and sleeping deeply on a chaise lounge in a pavilion on the edge of the lake in the book's English country house setting. I stripped off my sleeping pants, and I was lightly stroking my cock as I read of Hugh's character in his book sitting there and looking down at the sleeping man who was my character. Not being able to help himself, Hugh's character was lightly running his hands over the bare torso of my character.

As I read, I started to glide my hand over my belly and nipples just as was happening in the book. And the half-waking moaning of the character in the book came very much alive to me as my own arousing attention to my body brought out audible moans of my own. Hugh's character lowered his mouth to the tumescent manhood of his cousin's lover and started to gently work him to trembling arousal. In concert with that, I was stroking myself with increasingly rapid strokes. When Hugh entered a fully awake and accepting character of me in the book, I was entering myself with my own fingers, surfacing and mimicking images not only of the writing in the book but also of how Hugh had, in reality, so masterfully entered and worked my passage that fateful day in the cottage bedroom at Oakton Park.

The man in the pavilion was crying for the fucking of Hugh's character just as I was writhing in my bed, my attention prisoner to Hugh's fucking of me with the words in his book. The Hugh of the book ejaculated and the man in the pavilion cried his acceptance; I dropped the book, using both hands on myself now. Stroking hard with one hand, digging deep with the other. Thrashing about on the bed, working my hips wildly off and then back against the sheeting. And this time, when I at last found heavily fountained relief, it was Hugh's name I was crying out, not Luke's.

I read on through the night. I had to know how Hugh's book ended. I had to know if he saw any possible future for us in what had become such a complex, bittersweet saga. I was in tears when I reached the end, where some coincidence had brought the characters back together after a long parting, and the character who represented me was declaring how he had felt he just had to move on after Luke's death, that he couldn't let the character representing Hugh become a Luke substitute who was willing to accept him only to honor the memory of the dead lover.

"I am not the lover you came into my life with," Hugh's character said. "I am me. And I never was only willing, as you say, to accept you into my life and my bed because of what you and I once were to him. I wanted you because I fell in love with you. With you. I wanted you because my body aches to encase you and make love to you. And I agree that we both must move on from that shared tragedy in our lives. But that in no way means we need move away from each other; there's no reason why we need deny ourselves the pleasure of moving on together. Come to me. Come away with me."

The next day, the now-treasured copy of *Dead Lover's Gift* under my arm, I was at the travel agent's office making arrangements for a flight to Switzerland.

Coming for the Honey Man

I'd read the item in the *Intelligencer* social section incorrectly. It had been the first time I'd made this mistake, which led to the other mistakes. I made my living by playing the local newspapers on the Internet, figuring out where the rich suburbs were and something about the people living there, and watching for coming wedding announcements and evidence that there'd be empty houses stuffed with new wedding gifts as couples honeymooned far away. The Internet was a real blessing for this; it let me quickly pull together a long hit list of possibilities for any given area. A long list was necessary because all of the needed elements—absent owners, an unguarded house, and a big-pay stash—didn't come together that often.

And I needed a big-pay stash every couple of weeks, because I was high maintenance. I had a big appetite for fucking guys—a different guy each time—and they didn't come cheap.

I thought I'd hit pay dirt this time. Several months earlier I'd seen in the *Bucks County Intelligencer* what looked like several good prospects in a gentleman farmer county south of

Philadelphia, an area that was just dripping in cash. I could usually count on snobby places like this putting in announcements in their local papers at every step of the wedding ritual, and the *Intelligencer* hadn't disappointed me. I found engagement announcements that pinned down nearly a dozen weddings set for the time frame I was going to be in the Mid-Atlantic region. And using other articles in the on-line paper's business and social sections, I was able to pare these down to four possibilities for a big payoff.

The engagement announcements for three of those had been kind enough to let me know not only that the blissful couple already had a house to settle in, but also that they'd be honeymooning outside the States right after their wedding. Just a little more research and I'd picked out the wealthiest of these and had my target in sight, filed away my research, and went about my current business in the winter wedding wonderland of Aspen, Colorado.

* * * *

I parked my pickup truck in the dark shadow of some trees half a block away from the entrance into a tree-lined street of hulky graystone mansions, with DuPont green shutters. They were set comfortably apart from each other and the winding avenue, and I walked up to the house without anyone getting their feathers ruffled. I'd arrived the previous night and was staying at a motel in the suburbs of Wilmington, Delaware, just over the Pennsylvania line. If the caper was sniffed out before I managed to get out of the area altogether, I thought they'd be looking for me in Philadelphia rather than down there.

Although I was here in search of an empty house, as I stealthily approached, my thoughts went to what I had unexpectedly found here the previous day, the day of the wedding, when I had cased the house. I always like to get a sense of the layout of the target in daylight before I hit the house—and I'd found through experience that the second night was the best opportunity. On the day of the wedding, they usually thought well enough of the possibilities to station someone in the house during the ceremony and reception, and by the time everyone had recovered from the party, someone often came back to house sit. The night after the wedding, statistically, was always the best opportunity.

As I approached the house that night, my thoughts went ahead to the pleasantries of spending the money I planned to start raking in. Which led me to thoughts of the honey man. The warm June night was ideal for some action, and I was humming to myself and remembering his hair-rimmed left nipple and the way he had run his right hand around and across it as we had talked about the bees nesting on the house's wall. That memory, and my hand stroking over my dick through my pants, had me growing happily.

The previous day I had arrived early at the big stone house so typical of this area of Pennsylvania, and getting no answer after ringing the bell at the front door, had gone around to the side gate. I always approached the house in my casings openly and with a story I could tell if I unexpectedly found someone home. When I got to the side gate, I saw a head bobbing in the pool and called out, and the swimmer moved to the edge of the pool and lifted himself up out of the water.

"Ooohhheeeee." I whistled silently. The man was a real honey. I lifted the clipboard with the fake papers on it, ready to launch into my spiel about notification of delayed delivery on a wedding gift, when he made all of that unnecessary.

"So, are you the guy here about the bee hive Marion and Jim need to get rid of?"

"Ummm," I answered, not being quick on the uptake.

"I certainly hope you are," the honey man said. "Because I can't really stay waiting for this to be taken care of longer than tomorrow night. I need to be in Boston." All the time he was saying this, he was looking me up and down real carefully. I knew that look. He was interested. And I must say, he looked quite interesting to me too. Honey blond, honey lips, and a great swimmer's body.

"Sure, let me see the hive," I said.

He led me around to the side of the house, and sure enough, there was this large hive hanging off the side of the building slightly above head level, with a swarm of bees madly buzzing around it. I was about to say the wrong thing, when the honey man saved me again.

"It's a pity we can't just knock the hive off," he said. "But, with them being protected in this state, Marion and Jim had been looking all over for a beekeeper who would know how to move the hive away altogether. They're afraid the bees will get into the walls and then into the house."

"Yes, you have to handle them very carefully," I said wisely, giving the honey man the most welcome smile I could muster—and looking him up and down in that little Speedo of his so that he knew I was interested in more than the bees. "I have just what we need back in my truck. I got the address wrong; I'll have to go back down the street for it. But if you'll go back in the house, I'll get my equipment and have that hive away from here and going to a better place in no time."

"Oh good," he said. "And then come on into the house afterward." And the look he gave me told me I was as good as home as far as he and his type of honey was concerned.

I went back for the truck, and when I'd returned, I parked in the shadows near the side of the house, where there weren't any windows overlooking what I was doing. Then I took a baseball bat out of the back of the truck. I had the hive down and half way into the bushes at the side with one big swing. I retreated to the truck and waited for the bees to exhaust their anger, and then I came back and batted the hive deep into the undergrowth.

After being done with the bees, I went and rang the front doorbell again.

"All taken care of?" the honey man asked with his honey-mouthed smile when he answered the door. I'd thought he might have changed out of his Speedo while I was playing beekeeper. And he had, but he'd only changed into a towel wrapped around his waist.

"Yes, yes," I answered. "The little dears are all set up in a special compartment in my truck, all ready for a comfortable ride to their new home in a safer place with a great meadow full of pollen-filled flowers."

He was still giving me that lopsided grin ten minutes later when I had his back on the kitchen table and was grabbing his thighs and spooning my dipper inside his honey bucket. He was a little kinky and said he loved being surprised and wanted to be "taken," so I had his wrists bound with one tea towel over his head and around a table leg and his cries of passion muffled with another tea towel gagging his mouth. I fucked him hard for nearly a half hour, and he enjoyed it so much that he asked me to come back the next night. And, again, he set up the whole caper for me. This was the least amount of work I had to do and risk I had to take on a wedding burglary.

"I have to leave right afterward, though," he said at the door after one last kiss. "I've got to be back in Boston by the next morning." Perfect, I thought. Some entertainment and then he'll be gone and I can go about my intended business.

And then I was standing on the porch outside the front door, still holding the tea towels. My only regret was that, with the honey man right there all the time I was in the house, I didn't have an opportunity to scan and inventory the loot I'd be hauling in the next night after he took off for Boston.

* * * *

Now it was dark and I was early again. As the honey man had whispered in his instructions, I obediently walked up the long tree-shaded driveway toward the large attached garage. Now that it was night it was rather spooky. The trees made the drive black as black, in spite of the moon that was out, and in the background owls hooted. And things occasionally scuttled and rustled the vegetation. I hurried on with my attention to my cock slackening off in the surroundings.

Then I saw with relief that the garage was not far away, situated right at the end of the cream-colored gravel drive. I saw a figure moving about, going from the house to the garage. I smiled to myself at how eager the honey man was—that he'd wanted to have me inside him again even when he was so anxious to get off to Boston. I hurried on as quietly as I could and moved in to the partly open door of the garage and saw him open the Mercedes door, lighting up the interior, and leaning into the car, doing something inside. I moved in quietly to surprise him from behind, just as he told me he liked.

43

I pushed him forward and stripped his cotton pants down before kicking his legs apart, at the same time using one of the tea towels I'd brought back to gag him again. He was wriggling about but unable to cry out and wake the neighborhood. I held him down with a hand planted firmly between his shoulder blades and jerked my huge throbbing cock free and slid it back and forth over his entrance, my precum wetting it, but not enough for what I had in mind. But now I was just desperate to have him and didn't care about anything else. I added some spit and worked myself into his protesting honey pot of a hole, as he kicked uselessly and tried to worm his way free.

He had no luck. I was determined. I leaned in and fucked into him, finally making my limit inside his channel, my balls touching his butt. Then he was lying half in the car and half out, me bent kneed and standing outside the door and fucking into his tight passage, deep and hard.

When I'd come, I lay across the delicious honey man's back briefly, kissing his neck and shoulders while recovering my breath, as he moaned and mumbled inside his muffling gag. As I pulled back and withdrew from him and stood, he turned himself over and I found myself looking down at a stranger's face.

I was too shocked to do anything as he wrapped his legs about my hips, and I felt him pulling me back toward him. I was stunned. The man was not honey man. This new man was younger and more muscular. Now I thought he was going to trap me somehow to keep me there for some reason, maybe till the police came. Maybe he was a burglar, I suddenly thought. But no, I realized he had been wearing pajamas, and I had seen him myself, moving from the house to the garage. So he had to live there. I was the burglar, not him.

And now he was smiling up at me and drawing me toward him. He took my hand and led it down to his swollen cock. As I stroked him, I discovered he was trapping me so I had long enough for my tool to reengorge, so I could fuck him again. He wrapped a hand around me, and I bent over and kissed him on the eyelids and in the hollow of his neck. His other hand wrapping itself about my neck and pulling me in further, so that our half-hard cocks were stroking against each other and he moved his hand and held them like that, touching. I had my hands wrapped around his ass. Then I rose up and lifted his legs one at a time up so they rested on my shoulders and I had a good view of his puckered rim. He lifted one leg and braced himself against the interior roof of the car as his other leg continued to rest on my shoulder.

I had one finger at his entrance and worked it in as he arched and moaned. He watched me then, and I had to sink another, then a third one, before he began to pant behind his gag. His dick lay down his belly hard and jumpy and he played with the slit in his cap as I played inside his passage and my other hand stroked inside his thighs and over his belly and cupped his balls. I finger fucked him until he cried out in a muffled sound, shooting off up his belly and chest, and sending gobs on to the dashboard. Then as he went limp, I fed his hole my cock. He moaned and was watching me again as I fed it in and twisted and turned it as it went deeper. He moaned and whimpered and arched his back and widened his legs as I bottomed again inside him. This time I started slowly, with short fucks into the first few inches of his passage.

Our eyes were almost immediately locked, and I was completely lost in the fuck.

The sudden turning on of the garage lights shocked me again. I turned around with my cock still buried up the ass of the man lying half in, and half out of the car. He seemed completely unconcerned about the sudden illumination and just kept moving his hips in rhythm with my stalled fucking.

Turning, I saw that it was the honey man himself, standing there just inside the half open garage door with his hand on the light switch. The previous day's fuck had been so fast that I hadn't memorized his look. Still these two must at least be brothers.

"Marion," he was saying, not yet focusing on the Mercedes. "Since you and Jim are back early, I'd better be . . ."

And then he stood still in his tracks, taking my mistake completely in, his jaw dropped down to his chin.

Marion, I thought. Not Marian. Marion and Jim were both men.

I heard the gasping breathing from Marion as he jerked off the tea towel gag. He hadn't stopped the rhythm of his hips, fucking himself on my tool, however.

"You . . . go on . . . to Boston, Greg," he said in a hoarse voice. "Jim and I'll take care of this . . . intruder."

Just then another man walked into the garage from the drive. I have no idea what he had been doing while I fucked his Marion, but I was left in no uncertainly that he was the Jim who went with Marion, the dominating, big bruiser Jim. Marion's top.

I'd never been fucked before like Jim then took care of me while I continued plowing Marion and a disappointed honey man took his honey jar off to Boston. And it was several exhausting hours later that I discovered what my first mistake had been. I'd read the address wrong in the newspaper article. The wedding couple I had targeted lived in the next block.

Lying into the Future

Tomorrow. Bring your hands around my sides as I lay enveloped in your lap. Hold me in your hands until tomorrow, one hand cupping my balls, making me vulnerable to your touch, and the other hand possessing my cock closely—and stroke, stroke, stroke. Ahhhhhhh. Still cupping my balls with one hand, move the fingers of the other to my hole and invade and stretch, preparing me for you. Then at the stroke of tomorrow, turn me onto my belly, encase my thighs with your knees, and plunge into me with your firm cock, your palms pushing down on my shoulder blades, and ride me, ride me, r i d e m e . . . Ahhhhhhhhhh!

Poetry. The note from my absent lover, briefly back in New York to check on his financial affairs, was that and more to me. I sighed and turned off the computer and went to bed and lay in the dark, wondering how I had been so lucky as to end up with such a perfect lover.

Sheer chance. It had been a series of unconnected chances. The first time we had met had been half way up an alp in Switzerland. I laughed at the memory. Neither if us was serious climbers, but we had ended up meeting there. Hank was in a party on its way up, and I was in one on its way down. Both parties had stopped the night at the old timber and stone chalet perched on the side of the Matterhorn just before the climbing

47

began to get serious. I had sat off to one side by the fire in the main room as the others sat about talking about reaching the summit and the newcomers listened seriously.

But Hank had drifted over to me.

"So, how did you find the climb?" he asked.

"Me? I'm afraid I only made it as far as the next hut. I got the first signs of altitude sickness and wasn't interested in risking my life or anyone else's just to stand on top of a mountain. I'm not a serious climber, I'm afraid," I replied, wondering if he would make it, as he seemed older in years than the others in his team. Still he looked to be in superb shape, so perhaps he could outclimb the rest of them.

"I doubt I'll make it either," he said, smiling. "I used to climb when I was young, and my son decided this trip would be a great present for my birthday and something we could do together. I went up a practice mountain, not much more than a hill, really, with this group already, and I barely made it to the top of that."

"So, which one is your son?" I asked.

"He couldn't make it," he said. "His wife's about to have a baby. Their first. So he stayed home."

He was smiling a wide, honest smile, his dark eyes looking into mine and crinkled at the corners, his lips full and inviting. I shook my head to clear it of the sudden arousal he was causing in me. And I had to smile too.

"I was supposed to come with someone too. But he couldn't make it either," I told him. I had no idea why I had lied to him on that, though. I was here alone because my lover had died in an automobile wreck outside of Sydney just before the trip. But somehow I didn't want to tell this friendly and inviting—and desirable—stranger that. I thought then he'd only be fucking me out of sympathy.

We both smiled. I felt that, knowing we were both there alone, was causing a small sexual thrill to run between us. "They both wasted a lot of money." I said, "and it means I've got a room to myself," I added, hoping Hank was thinking the way I was. After a week's climbing—alone when I hadn't planned to be alone—I was feeling both on-the-edge vulnerable and randy.

He looked over at the main crowd. "I don't think anyone will notice our absence," he said. "But the blond giant over there is from my town back home so . . . ," he trailed off.

"So we'd better be quick," I added, getting up and moving to the passageway that led to the ground floor rooms. In a moment Hank was behind me in the dim passage, pressing up close and running his hands over my torso and my hips.

I opened the door to my room, and we landed against the back of it as it closed. He kissed me, and I sucked his tongue in and pulled him in hard. His thick rod pressing against my hip as mine moved against his belly. He was unbuttoning my pants and pushing them down as our mouths wrestled in the way I liked. Strong and demanding. Eager and hot. Then he was on his knees, his head of steel gray hair sinking over my engorging rod. His dark eyes looked up at me in a lost way as he tongued my cap and stroked my length. Then he did a good job of swallowing me, and I lay my head back and moaned loudly, a moan of release and need as I enjoyed the first good mouth on my dick I'd had for weeks.

I had thought he would be the dominant one, but once I was throbbing and gripping his hair as I fucked into his throat and gazed into his eyes, he pulled back. I was confused as he came in for a kiss and pulled me back toward the narrow bed. Then he fell back and was stripping off his jeans. I pulled them free as he kicked off his briefs and lifted his legs wide. His eyes were begging me to fuck him as his cock bounced against his belly, and he gripped it and tugged his balls and stroked himself. I fingered his hole, and he wrapped his legs about my back and pushed his hips up now, saying, "Yes, yes. That feels so good."

I held his hips and fed my tool down into his hole as he watched it disappear, groaning and moaning, then crying out in small held-back cries as I stroked shallowly inside him. He came in a fountain that landed over his chest and face. I sunk deep to the limit inside him and plowed him briefly and then pulled out, shooting my load across him, my cum landing on top of his on his chest and belly. His legs dropped, and I fell onto him, and we kissed again deeply and slowly.

In a few minutes he pulled away, though, and cleaned himself up at the basin in the room as I lay on the bed and watched him.

"So, why didn't your friend come?" he asked, making conversation to cover the embarrassment of us both that we had fucked within minutes of meeting each other. I wasn't the kind to do that, and I didn't think Hank was that kind either.

I looked away, wanting to keep this meeting simple and not wanting him to see the pain of the lie on my face. "He decided he'd rather be living by the beach in Hawaii with blonds twenty years younger than me," I said, hoping he wouldn't pursue the point and catch me out in the convenient lie.

Hank stopped in the middle of sponging the cum off his shirt. "Oh," he said, locking his eyes briefly to mine in the small mirror over the basin, before dropping his gaze again. "I'm sorry," he finally said. And I sucked in my breath from the way he said it, almost as if he could look straight through me to the truth.

I shrugged, and tried to bolster the lie. "After six months, I'm starting to get used to being on my own again."

"Well, I'd better get back before I'm missed," he said, tucking his shirt back into his pants and running his fingers through his hair to smooth it.

There was no farewell kiss, and in a moment he had slipped out of the door and was gone. I threw on my dressing gown and headed to the showers to clean up. Then I crawled into bed and spent too long trying to forget how much I missed having a man I wanted to be with around all the time.

In the morning his party had left on the upward climb before I was even up.

* * * *

I had lied to Simon about my son booking this mountain-climbing trip for my birthday and then reneging because his wife was having a baby. My lover had booked the trip—and paid for it too—and then I had found him in bed with my driver. I had taken this trip for revenge. I had taken both tickets and boarded the flight the next morning, not because I had wanted to come here alone—I hadn't been the one who wanted to come here at all—but simply to make Russ pay. He had lived off me in so many respects and for so long that I was determined to get a little back and to make him pay if he was going to cheat on me.

And I had continued to take my revenge. Russ had cheated on me, so I was doing everything I could in the way of payback. I had flaunted myself in front of all of the other men in our climbing party. The trip had been booked through a gay travel agency, so I wasn't worried that the men might not be interested. And I had taken them on one after the other—sometimes two of them at once. I had saved the best for last—the blond giant I'd told Simon was from my home town. He wasn't from my home town. He was some Scandinavian who, as far as I knew, could speak no more English than the phrase "I want to fuck you."

I had told Simon our tryst would have to be a short one, because this was the Scandinavian's evening with me. I'd finally learned the Norwegian words for "OK, let's fuck tonight."

I have no firm idea why I lied to Simon about everything when we'd met. He was so nice and friendly and had been so open and honest with me. I think it might have been because he instantly reminded me of Russ—of the best parts of Russ that I could remember. And I was still so wounded by what Russ had done. But I also still ached for Russ. I went with Simon that day, I think, because I still ached for Russ, no matter what he'd done to me. And I also lied to Simon, I believe, because I was ashamed for him to think I would open my legs just for anyone—although that's exactly what the desire for revenge against Russ's transgression had led me to on this trip.

After I left him and found the blond giant and let him manhandle me on the squeaking bed in his room, pumping and pumping me until we were afraid the bed frame would fall through the floor to the room below, I tried to forget Simon—to push him out of my mind. But he was so much like the Russ I had first loved. My climbing party was half way up to the base camp hut the next day before I realized that I didn't want to leave Simon that way—perhaps that I didn't want to leave him at all.

I had gotten his business address in Sydney, and I spent most of the next year putting my affairs in New York in order so that I could be gone for a large chunk of time. This would have been a far easier chore if I'd still had my driver . . . and my accountant, Russ.

* * * *

Eight months later I bumped into Hank as I was buying a gelati cone from the ice cream counter at the Opera House end of the row of shops that ran under Circular Quay station in Sydney.

I felt a touch on my shoulder and turned around. The face of the man behind me looked familiar. But I couldn't place it and just stared blankly.

He looked uncertain. "I'm sorry, you look like someone I met on an alp in Switzerland," he said apologetically.

Then it fell into place.

"Hank," I said, smiling at him in pleasant remembrance. "The Chalet. You going up; me down."

"Yes," he said with a sigh of obvious relief at not having made an idiot of himself. "But I rather think I mostly lay there and you went up and down," he added in a whisper, and then gave a nervous little laugh as we both blushed in remembrance.

I got my ice cream and we moved away from the crowded counter.

"A small world," he said, looking me over appraisingly. "You look good."

"And you," I answered, still feeling awkward at having a casual conversation like this with a stranger I'd known so fully and deeply. "What are you doing here?"

"My son again," Hank answered. "But this time he and his wife are with me. Over there," he said, turning and pointing at a young dark-haired couple with a stroller.

"We've been here for a week, and it's our last day, so we came to have another ride on a ferry in the harbor again. And you? You live here?" he asked.

"No. I did live here, but now I live up the coast," I said. "I'm just here for the day. I had to check into my business in

Manly. If it wasn't so hot, I would have gone straight back," I said, indicating the melting ice cream I held.

He pulled my ice cream-filled hand to him and dipped his head to lick slowly and suggestively up the cone as he looked into my eyes.

I almost laughed out loud it was so corny, but the look in his eyes had my dick jumping, and I kept my mouth closed. It was the sweetest offer I had had in a long time.

"Let me go speak to my son and his wife for a moment, and then I'll come back to you . . . if you want me to," he said. I couldn't tell him no. I said nothing, and he got the message.

I watched as he went over to the couple and talked to them very briefly and then came back to me.

"May, my daughter-in-law, wants to head back, Ray said, as it's about time for Fay's nap, and I haven't much time. I need to get on the Net and get some work done before the office opens back home. So, why don't you show me to someplace private?"

I led the way to the nearest hotel, only to find it was fully booked. We moved to the next one and same story. We found out that there was a Lions Club convention in town, the annual international one, and apparently every hotel in town was full.

We could have found somewhere, I was sure, but I took it as a sign.

"Well, I think I am going to have to show you Sydney instead," I said. He looked disappointed, but I realized I was mainly ready to give up looking because I was getting tired of hurried casual sex.

Instead, we went to the Museum of Contemporary Art, and by the time we left, we both knew that we had similar taste and were quite comfortable in each other's company. Then it was the design center, a coffee, and on to the huge steel bolts that connected the Sydney Harbor bridge to its stone moorings. We walked along the edge of the harbor and talked and finished up at a small restaurant ready for another coffee and talked some more. Hank called his son and said we'd be having dinner together and he'd be back after that.

After dinner, we strolled back toward Circular Quay, and as we passed under the moorings of the bridge, Hank walked up the grassy slope into the shadows of the bridge's stone foundations and pulled me with him. It was Tuesday and there was no one about, and he pulled me into the dark shadows thrown across the grass by the bridge. Then he silently lay back on the slope and pulled me down with him.

As we kissed, I unzipped him and reached in for his rod and pulled it free, and he unzipped me and pulled mine free as he shimmied his hips and slipped his own pants down. Somehow our lips remained connected as I sunk my cock inside him.

I plowed him in silence, just the lapping of the water and the muted city noises in the background. I plowed him deeply and slowly, and we came together as a train rumbled overhead, drowning my cry of release, me deep inside him and him soaking my belly. I lay there on top of him as I softened inside him, his hands running all over me, our mouths joined again.

We were still brushing off the grass and giggling like teenagers as we returned to the footpath, trying to look as if nothing had happened.

* * * *

I was sure now. I had wanted to be sure. If Simon hadn't been muttering that he loved me while we fucked and wasn't giving me that sad expression now at the prospect of leaving off again, I wouldn't have had the strength to go on. But I was sure now, so I did.

"So, do you have anyone waiting for you at home up the coast?" I asked. I tried to keep my voice light and off hand, but this was possibly the second most important question of my life that I had to ask.

"No, No. No one at all," he answered somewhat wistfully.

And with that I moved on to the most important question of my life, "Would you mind terribly having someone at home waiting for you when you came down to Sydney?"

He stopped abruptly and turned to me and looked deeply into my eyes. I could hardly make him out, though, because my eyes were misting over. I was trembling and trying quite unsuccessfully to put a brave face on just how important this moment was to me.

He did understand my meaning, though. And with misting eyes of his own, he took my arm in his and pulled in close and said, quietly, "No, I don't think I'd mind terribly at all. Not at all. In fact, that would be very nice."

We walked in silence for several minutes, each of us struggling to control our emotions.

But then he spoke again. "But what of your son and his wife and the child back there? Can you just—?"

I cut him off with a nervous little laugh. "Oh them. I don't know them from Adam. I don't have a son; I don't have any children. I just asked them for the time when I went over to them back there. They were just part of my escape mechanism if you said you wouldn't have me."

He was still in confusion, but he hadn't let loose his clutching hold on my arm as we continued to stroll into the future. I did, though, make a mental note that I'd best stop telling him these gigantic lies.

Captain's Obsession

The invitation was engraved, which of course it would be, but it was addressed to me specifically. One open invitation to the consulate staff and then this separate one for only me. I was only the U.S. vice consul in Naples, Italy. So why my own invitation? I separated it out and slipped it into my suit coat pocket as I moved toward the consul's office. Alice would not be pleased if she saw that I'd gotten a specific invitation and she, the consul, hadn't.

But when I got to Alice's office, she only had eyes for me. She showed no interest in the mail at all. She was giving me those doe-eyed, swimming in semen adoring looks of hers that I hoped the rest of the staff didn't see. Her eyes were asking for more of the same of what I'd given her the previous night, rapid piston action to the depths of her writhing, moaning body on her living room carpet. Maybe tonight we'd make it as far as the bed. Or whatever she wanted. She was calling the shots.

The invitation was for the USS *Chester Lenox*, a U.S. *Arleigh Burke*–class Aegis guided missile destroyer, that would be appearing for a courtesy port call and a show of the American flag in Naples Bay in three-days' time. Per protocol there would be a cocktail party for local dignitaries on the destroyer's fantail, and, of course, I and the rest of the staff of the American consulate in Naples would be invited to that—and would be expected to show up and fawn over the local dignitaries.

Which all didn't explain the personal invitation sent only to me. I had spent my two years aboard ship in the navy, but I'd been a lowly seaman. Surely that would not be what would get me my own invitation.

The day of the cocktail reception was glorious, and I had an exhilarating feeling of the best of the days I spent in the navy cutting through the foam of the sea with a cruiser under my feet as the launch streaked its way through the yachts in the harbor and out to the U.S. destroyer hunkering majestically and malevolently in the center of the bay. I could feel the raw power and sensuality of the hulking structure of the boat and felt myself aroused. Alice must have done so as well, as she put her hand on my thigh, supposedly to steady herself in the lurching launch, but the look in her eye told me, "See that sleek vessel of power and brute force we are approaching? That is you between my legs—my own guided missile destroyer." Ah, the things we do to progress in our careers.

We were handed up to fantail of the Chester Lenox, where the party was already in full bloom in a swirl of black tuxedos, brightly colored cocktail dresses, navy whites, clinking glasses, and lilting laughter. We were guided to the reception line, me immediately behind Alice.

"Dr. Alice Worthington, U.S. consul general to Naples," a protocol officer at the captain's elbow carefully enunciated.

My attention had been diverted to admiring the sleek lines of this new class of destroyer, but all of my senses snapped right back to the reception line as the protocol officer continued.

"Dr. Worthingon. May I introduce the commanding officer of the USS *Chester Lenox*, Captain Theodore Sims."

I was paralyzed and speechless. The naval attaché at the consulate had to nudge me to take up my place in front of the captain as Alice moved on. She was already being asked what she would like to drink by a handsome young blond navy lieutenant, all big-toothed smiles and well-cut muscle, who was guiding her with one hand on her elbow and the other waving to a seaman with an hors d'oeurves tray balanced in his hand.

"Matthew Crenshaw, vice consul general—"

"We've already met," the captain cut in. "Mr. Crenshaw was in the navy. He's already served under me. Hello, Matt."

I had trouble focusing my attention, maintaining my demeanor, and finding a voice.

"Hello, Ted . . . I mean Captain Sims. Welcome to Naples." I felt so exposed. That "he's already served under me" said so much; it said it all. I was surprised that those around us were able to keep straight faces. But of course they wouldn't know. Or wouldn't they? He ruled a ship now. I couldn't believe he would have changed. Some of these naval guys in his command surely knew. The invitation. At least this now explained my personal invitation.

"I'd like a moment with you later, if you will, Matt," the captain was saying. I could do no more than nod my head and then I was gone, beyond the line and milling around in the swarm of partygoers, most of them there for the free food and drink and the glow of having been invited and, more important, being seen to have been invited.

For several moments I was lost in the swirling revelers in a world of my own—a world of vivid memories. My last night in the navy on board the cruiser in the Persian Gulf. Assigned that last night for watch duty on the starboard in the shadows of the bridge. The dark Greek muscle hunk executive officer, Lieutenant Ted Sims, coming up close behind me at the rail. He had pursued me for months, but I was only a seaman and he was second in command—and he was so overpowering. I was terrified of the possible ramifications of that—for both of us.

But he was here, close behind me, my last night. Whispering in my ear of his need; his anger and frustration that I had eluded him until it almost was too late. His wanting me. The massiveness of his cock rubbing against the small of my back screamed of his desire. Me, pushed up against the rail, my arms splayed out, his fists holding my wrists in bondage, his hot breath on my neck, his words invading me, arousing me, his massive chest digging into my shoulder blades, his cock rubbing up and down on the small of my back and between my butt cheeks through the thin cotton of my shorts.

I began to tremble and whimper, and he could tell the instant I had given in to him. He pushed my shorts down in

59

back and rubbed his cock across my hole, one of his hands went under my T-shirt hem and slithered up to my nipples and the other pushed down past the waistband of the shorts and found and encased and squeezed and stroked me. He was still breathing heavily at my ear, his lips buried in my neck, and he was whispering of how he had to punish me for making him wait so long and for there being so little time now.

Lost in him now, I turned my face to his and signaled my surrender to him by passionately returning his kiss on my lips. But that wasn't enough for him. He invaded my mouth with his fingers and told me to lather them up well. And then he was fingering my hole with them, lubricating me and opening me to him. He had the bulging head of his dick against my hole, but he stopped, poised there. I was already groaning and gulping with mixed anticipation.

"You. You have to initiate it," he was murmuring to me. "You have to show me it's what you want." Then he took my right hand from the rail, stilling gripping it hard by the wrist, and moved it to between our pelvises, to his engorged tool. He made me hold his cock to my hole and then move my butt back onto it. He made me force the entry, with great pain and panting and moaning. But then, once it was a couple of inches inside me, he plunged and plunged and plunged. And I threw my head back and yelled to the sky, the cries of my taking lost in the thundering of the foam in the surging Persian Gulf waters.

" . . . the U.S. stock market will—"

"Excuse me? Excuse me, what was that you said? The noise, you know—" I was peddling as fast as I could to return to the here and now of the cocktail party. The deputy mayor of Naples, whose favorite topic was the health of the U.S. stock market that he was so heavily invested in, was mining me for insider information I didn't have, even though he seemed never able to grasp that reality.

"I said, do you think the U.S. stock market will rebound in the next quarter?" He was looking at me with such concern and intensity that I felt I had to say something. That was my job here in Naples; keeping everyone happy with the United States, American tourists and local businessmen alike. And captains of visiting U.S. naval vessels, for that matter.

"I . . . I think—" I started, but then I was saved by the ship's protocol officer. He had his white-gloved hand on my sleeve and was cutting in with his smooth but authoritative voice.

"Excuse me, sir. I'm so, so sorry, but the captain has asked to have a word with Mr. Crenshaw in private. He'll be just a moment. I'll return him straightaway."

The protocol officer led me through a hatch doorway just below the bridge and then backed out of the door. When it had clinked shut, Ted appeared from a side doorway and encased me in his arms. He kissed me deeply, and I could tell that he was just as tense and angry he had been on that last night when he fucked me against the rail of the cruiser.

"All that time you lost us," he said through clenched teeth when he'd come up for breath. "You gave me months of frustration."

"Ted, Ted," I said. "That was long ago—We can't—"

"I want you to follow this gangway back to the room beyond that door at the end and wait for me there. I won't be long." And then he was gone.

Ted was such a forceful presence. I had always tried to keep my distance because I'd known I could not resist his gravitational pull. And he was such a consuming and commanding force that I was afraid of him and of his effect on me. I knew I couldn't fight him here and now, on his own ship, and so I slowly moved down the corridor toward the closed door at the far end.

The passage was poorly lit, and quite unexpectedly an arm emerged from a partly open bulkhead off to the left, and grabbing hold of the diaphanous shirt of my summer tuxedo, yanked me sideways. Doubly stunned now, before I could react to this new surprise, I was pulled into a cabin and the door was closed with a final metallic clang.

Inside the space only a dull red nightlight illuminated the windowless gloom, and I saw shadows swirling around me; hands reaching for my body and finding it. The shadows came in closer and surrounded me. They were carefully but completely disrobing me. I was blind beyond the sense of motion around me, but there were things I could hear. I could hear rasping

61

breaths, small gasps, and moans, as the big strong, long-fingered hands of the shadowy figures glided over the curves of my body and found my tender, exposed parts.

Mouths descended on my mouth. And I tasted the intimate inner taste of their owners. Some sweet, some smoky, some tasting of wine. Other mouths found my skin, and I was lathered in saliva and damp heat as the tongues caressed me. Tongues followed the lines of my veins and arteries, delved into the creases of my armpits, flowed along the sides and over the head of my manhood, invaded the crevice leading deep inside me.

One voice was repeatedly crying out now in arousal, and I suddenly realized that it was my voice. Bodies were covering mine in a writhing entwining, and I tried desperately to move up in the swirling pile. I climbed above the others but was dragged relentlessly back into the center of the undulating mass, as the searching hands and probing fingers delved into the crevices of my body and found hidden tender parts.

Then I ceased to hear myself as another mouth possessed mine, and my body was stretched and spread and tied and opened, and made ready to be entered by the hard throbbing tools of my captors. Big, long, hot, throbbing cocks pushing at my mouth, sliding in my armpits, rubbing across my chest and belly, being encased with mine and stroked, invading my hole. Plunging and pumping, and going rigid, and flowing. Being withdrawn, only to be replaced again different invaders, all throbbing, all, in the end, flowing. I sank into unconsciousness.

When I awoke, I was splayed out naked on the floor of a small, private, minimally functional but pristine clean head, and my clothes were neatly folded and sitting on the toilet seat. I arose with the groans of stiffness screaming at me, showered in the small stall, and methodically, painfully redressed over bruised skin and stretched muscle. Then, putting on my best "nothing happened here; no making of waves here" diplomatic face, I found my way back to the fantail.

The party was breaking up. Alice had already left—or was leaving. I reached the rail in time to see her looking up at me from the launch with a perplexed, questioning look in her eyes. The blond lieutenant was sitting beside her in the launch.

"Don't worry. She will be well serviced tonight," Ted said as he sauntered up beside me close at the rail. "I told her we had wanted to entertain you on board for the evening and would return you to work in the morning. I could tell from her reaction that she was expecting you to be available tonight. You needn't do your duty tonight, though. The lieutenant will give her a good ride—as I will give you."

That night, as I lay spread-eagled on the bed in the captain's cabin, my white-knuckled hands gripping notches in the headboard overhead tightly, my legs spread wide, a pillow under the small of my back, me crying out my consumed passion, and a hard and grunting Ted crouched between my thighs and plunging again and again deep inside me, I felt the change in him. He no longer exuded the anger and frustration he had during our fleeting fuck on the cruiser or his kiss in the gangway. Now he was just enjoying me—and I had to admit, now that he somehow had exacted his little obsession for revenge, that I was enjoying him too.

Misunderstandings

I leant my hip against the veranda rail and drank my coffee as I gazed out over the green of the mountains and the string of houses nestled in the trees along the shore. All reflected back to me in the silver mirror that was the early-morning lake.

When I'd finished my coffee, I wandered back inside and into the kitchen. Hank was there, wearing nothing but a pair of running shorts while consulting a recipe book and frowning. I dipped my finger into the beaten contents of the large mixing bowl standing on the bench beside him, and then I reached over and smeared the cake mix around his right nipple. Hank yelped and turned, making it easier for me to spread it in the dark hair and over the hard brown knob.

"Hey," he laughed, as I bent to suck the sweet cake mix off the hairs surrounding his dark nub and large aureole. Licking them clean, tasting the salt under the sweet goo. Feeling his nipple harden and his breathing get faster. Meanwhile, my cake mix-coated finger was moving to his left nipple and spreading the mixture over that dark spray of hair and the exposed skin.

I lapped and sucked that one clean too, my cock stiffening as I ran the last of the mix down to his quivering belly and followed it with my tongue. My own tool began to press against the material covering it, and my hand finally slipped into his shorts and grasped the root of his cock. I slowly slipped my hand along his engorging length, loving the growing firmness of him as I pulled his seven inches free of his shorts. My tongue stretched out to his cap and I tasted him there. Yum.

"Uh, oh." Hank gasped as his hands moved to my head. "Give me five minutes," he croaked, pulling my head up and bringing our mouths together. "I have to get this in the oven soon, or it wont be any good for tonight."

We had visitors coming for dinner. Our mouths joined in a deep kiss, and I pulled him to me and we rubbed our stiffening cocks together briefly, both already hard and eager.

"OK," I replied in a growl, "Five minutes. And if you aren't lying naked on the bed by then, I'll be coming after you," I added, smiling. Looking into his dark, laughing, incredibly sexy eyes. "Yum. Have I told you lately how good you taste?" I asked, in my deepest voice.

"Frequently," he told me huskily, "Now go. Or this cake will be ruined."

* * * *

There had been no life for me before there was Sandy. I had thought I was getting along fine, but I was wrong.

I had always thought of myself as an asexual sort of guy. I had been lost in my studies and then my job, not even realizing that there was anything else to life, when I'd been enticed to go on that blind date I refer to as "the disaster." We were parked at a seaside lookout point in my new convertible—I later suspected I only was along because of that convertible. Ned was in the backseat with his date, and I heard them going at each other hot and heavy. Then the girl I had been tagged with started rubbing up against me in the front seat and running her hand between my legs. The blood rushed to my ears—I could hear that over the noise of the surf below us. I panicked. And that ruined the evening. It wasn't until years later that I realized that all of my senses that evening were tuned into the sounds of lust that Ned was making there in the backseat.

How was I to know, though? My parents were cold people. They never touched each other that I could see. They certainly didn't touch me. It was all striving ambition for them. For me as well as them.

I didn't know until Sandy came along anything about myself, really. I only discovered myself—my wants and desires and capabilities—slowly. Slowly, as his cock entered me that first time and filled me and thrilled me and moved endlessly inside me. I had never known what a moan of pleasure was until I was nearly twenty-five.

And if it hadn't been for the misunderstandings, I probably still wouldn't know.

The cake that day. And I laugh about this. I was proud of my cakes. Vain, really. That dinner party was important to me. There was a lot of time and effort and money invested in that cake. And yet, when I heard the sound of the timer telling me it was done, I didn't care. Fuck the cake was all I could think. Sandy was arched over me, kissing me on the lips and the eyes, and in the hollow of my neck, while his hard, hard cock was moving ever deeper inside me. Fuck the cake was all I could think. And fuck the dinner party, if it came to that. I would be here, my legs spread wide for my lover for just as long as he was moving deep inside me.

We made do with almost-stale ice cream.

* * * *

I remember it was a Tuesday. Not Monday. No idea why, as I have a bad memory for days and dates. I can't remember the date. The month, yes. It was August. Late. So it was a Tuesday in late August.

The guy who had been behind the counter came over with the bill. "I'm sorry we're closing now," he said, and I had looked up and seen that the small café was empty. Except for me.

"Sorry," I said vaguely, and stood up, finding I was unsteady on my feet as I fished out my wallet and put $50 into his hand.

"Enough?" I asked, feeling the full effects of the bottle of wine I had had with my late meal.

"I'll get your change," he replied, and moved off.

"Keep it," I mumbled, feeling like giving it all away.

My life was in ruins and money was a minor thing just at that moment.

I shuffled out onto the street, and the heat hit me. A hot damp evening. No, night. It was very late, and the usually busy road was empty; not a cab in sight, and I ended up walking all the way back to my apartment by the river. Revived by the fresh air. I often walked home. That was why I lived there, it was only a fifteen-minute walk to Morton Grey Developments.

At the entry door, I bumped into a guy leaving. He was dark and lean, but strong looking and masculine with it, and pulling some sort of small bag on wheels. He smiled slightly as he passed me, and somewhere in my fuzzy mind it registered that he appealed to me and that it was a long time since I had fucked anyone. Even longer since it had been really memorable. I turned to watch him walk to the edge of the road as a cab pulled up, and I stood and watched him get in and be driven away. He looked back at me briefly, and then I turned away and went in through the main entry door and forgot him.

Morton Grey Developments. I worked there. And on that Tuesday I had found my career collapsing into ruins. That was why I was crawling home late. That was why I had gone out to eat and had too much wine over a late dinner eaten alone. That was why I saw him—the first time.

At Morton Grey we had our weekly progress meetings on Tuesday mornings. And that morning Dave had bypassed me and handed our big new project to Malcolm Morrison. Malcolm had joined us six months before, coming over from a large private developer specializing in luxury retirement projects.

"It looks like Forest Lake is going ahead," Dave had said, and a murmur of approval went around the table.

The project was big and had come up against some environmental problems that had seen the design team reworking it for the last two years. I had been sitting back at the meeting, needing something new to get my teeth into and waiting hungrily for Dave to put it my way. I got all the hard ones, and the really big ones. Ever since I had first come to Morton Grey, I had been focused on being the only choice to take over Dave's job when he retired.

Instead, he had looked at Malcolm, and said, "Malcolm, I think that Forest Lake will benefit from your experience at Paradise Cove."

Surprised murmurs rippled around the table, and I went cold, and my smile froze.

A few minutes later he handed me Milson Park, a small inner-city development. Very small by our standards. A nothing project by mine, I thought.

"And Sandy, call my wife," he added, looking right at me, "She wants to talk to you about the weekend."

"I hope you aren't too upset about Dave giving the Forest Lake project to Malcolm," she said, after some desultory small talk.

I wasn't shocked she was behind the decision. I knew Dave relied heavily on her advice in some things. I just felt hurt and betrayed.

"Why?" I asked, clenching my fist, my anger showing through in my voice.

"Its time you did something but work, Sandy. It's four years now since Lars . . . died. I'm sorry, but someone has to say it. To do something. There's more to life than work. And, anyway, Milson Park is special. You'll like working on it."

"I wanted Forest Lake," I replied stonily, and there was a few moments silence.

"Do you do anything but exercise at the gym and work? Tell me, honestly."

"That's not the point," I replied angrily.

Lars. There was hardly a day I didn't think of him. He'd worked in the emergency department of the local hospital and had died there. Stabbed repeatedly in the neck by a drug-crazed patient he had been attending to.

Rebecca and Dave had been more supportive than anyone else afterward, and I owed them both. I'd had nightmares regularly in the first year. Seeing Lars in a pool of blood, me struggling helplessly to stop it, waking exhausted and in tears.

That Tuesday had dragged, and I had left work depressed. Part of me knew that Rebecca was right. But most of me didn't want to admit it or deal with it. I decided my life was a mess, and after sitting alone in my flat—which had been Lars's and mine—I felt even more depressed and had finally gone out to have something to eat. And I had walked home more drunk than sober.

On Friday I took a walk over to the site for Milson Park. And there my work brain took over. I suddenly saw that it might be a small project, but that in its own small way, it was as challenging as Forest Lake. And it was probably the most exclusive project we had ever built. The half dozen residences were all spread over several levels at different angles, which maximized privacy and views. Looking at the plans and the site, I could see that the architect had done a great job. His name wasn't familiar; he was someone new, not someone I had worked with before.

But the site had problems with access and the slope of the site was difficult, and I knew that it was going to take up a lot of my time for such a small-sounding project. And I'd need to work closely with the architect. I wasn't sure that some of what he had in mind was going to be practical.

On Saturday night, I went to Rebecca's party. I had tossed up the idea of not going, but knew that was petty. I owed her and Dave too much. So, instead, I arrived on the dot at 7 pm.

Rebecca made a fuss of me, and as few other guest were there yet, she dragged me into the study and gave me her new "you need to get out and find someone" lecture. I mumbled and got annoyed, but I tried not to let it show. I downed a strong drink, and as soon as she released me, I wandered to the bar and got another. I usually didn't drink more than the odd glass of wine.

I knew nearly all the faces at the party. I went to most of their parties, and had done so for years. When I first started at Morton Grey, I had hesitated to take Lars the first time I was invited, but he had insisted. And we had been accepted as a couple without comment. Fortunately, Malcolm wasn't there today. I wasn't sure how I would have dealt with that. But it wasn't a party for the staff, it was more of a family party.

At some stage I saw a face I recognized, but was surprised to see, and couldn't quite place. By then I was feeling rather mellow and was certainly not sober and the party was quite noisy. Then Dave brought the familiar stranger over and introduced him. "Sandy, I want you to meet Frank, he. . . . ," Dave said more, but it was lost in a sudden shout of laughter and the general hubbub, and I smiled and shook hands and said "Hi." and Dave moved off.

"Nice party," I said, almost shouting. "Where do I know you from?" I asked. I recognized Frank, but still couldn't place him. But he had given me an encouraging look over, and I found him surprisingly appealing.

"Rebecca," Frank replied, and I could hear his American accent, over the noise of the party, as he continued talking. "I've been taking cocks, four of them, all day. A mixture. They came out well."

I had no idea what he was talking about, and to be honest I was shocked at his openness, but it sounded incredibly hot and I liked the look of him and I was half drunk. And the last few days with time on my hands I was suddenly feeling hornier than I had for months.

I leaned in and put my mouth to his ear, "So do you want to take my cock too? Fuck all night?" I asked.

Frank jumped back and went red and gave me an odd look. "I don't think so," he said coldly and turned and walked off.

Great butt I thought, as he moved away, shame he's such a stuck up slut. The party moved on, and I got a bit drunker and then got into the birthday cake. It was more than good. Rebecca told me it was her nephew Hank's special Milky Way cake.

"He bakes all the cakes for me," she said, "he's very versatile."

I didn't know about the versatility, but he could certainly make a great cake. I was ready to go before the party started to break up, and when I found Rebecca to say good-bye, she was talking to the very hot and good-looking, well-fucked, but stuck-up slut Frank.

"I'm off," I said, moving in to give Rebecca a kiss.

Rebecca hugged me, "You may as well share a taxi with Hank then," she said. "He's ready to go and he's temporarily living in your apartment building."

"Ok," I said, shrugging, having no idea which one Hank was, and not really caring, "I'll go and call the cab then."

As I ordered the cab, I saw Rebecca having a tense discussion with Frank.

"It's coming; I'll wait outside." I told her when I had finished the call.

"Hank will go with you," she said, and pushed Frank forward and left us.

"But. I thought you were Frank," I said, wondering how drunk I was.

"No. I'm Hank," he replied coldly.

"Oh," I said, "Rebecca said . . . oh, you are the guy who lives in my apartment building," I added foolishly, suddenly remembering where I had seen him before—our previous meeting at the entry door to the apartment building.

"Yes," he replied.

The cab came and we got in and rode silently into the city. I saw his hand covering his lap and was sure he had an erection, and was getting a bit sick of his coolness and superior look. And I was horny and angry and annoyed with Rebecca and. . . . And well lots of things. Like half drunk.

As soon as we were inside the entrance to the building, I pushed Frank, Hank, whatever, up against the wall, and, with my face right in his, I said, "You couldn't resist telling me you were getting fucked all day today. By four guys. And how good it turned out. So how come you don't want to be fucked all night? Or is your boyfriend waiting for you?" At the same time I grabbed his mound, surprised at the size of his growing dick, and I squeezed it.

"You're mad," he gasped, "I did not tell you anything like that. Get off."

Hank pushed me harder than I expected, and I staggered back, still feeling his stiffening dick in my now-empty hand.

"I told you I had been baking cakes all day. Baking. I made Rebecca's birthday cake, and the three others, the carrot cake, the yellow cake, and a coconut cake. You're a lunatic, with a serious drinking problem. And don't you ever touch me again," he added, shaking with anger and glaring at me, before he turned and sprinted up the stairs and out of sight.

A few moments later I heard a door bang closed somewhere up above me. I looked at the empty stairs, my cock staining at my pants, my hand still hot from the heat of his mound, my open mouth desperate to taste his.

"Shit," I said out loud. "Shit."

* * * *

That first encounter with Sandy, that first misunderstanding-based encounter was when my life started. I know that now. Before that, I hadn't lived. I was as cold as ice—as frigid and as dead on my feet as my parents were. I gauge my life in two parts: before and after Sandy's cock entered me. The first part a cold death, the second part hot, hot overflowing of life, the scorching, freeing, imprisoning feel of the hot poker searing my insides, melting me, branding me as alive in the very center of me.

But those two parts don't divide so evenly. That awkward pass he made at me in a drunken stupor in the foyer of our apartment building. That was the beginning of the beginning. He cradled my penis through the thin fabric of my trousers, the first time since that unfortunate blind date in my convertible that anyone had touched me there. And although it enraged me, it also inflamed me. I didn't consciously process it at that moment, but somewhere, somewhere deep inside me, I knew that I wanted that hand there. That I wanted much more than that. I wanted to be writhing underneath this man as he thrust inside me and moved in and out, endlessly.

I stumbled up the stairs to my apartment, and, as I had done on many a lonely night, I lay on my bed, naked, and stroked myself. But whereas before I never dreamt of anything while I was masturbating other than relief followed by untroubled sleep, this night I dreamt of Sandy fucking me as I masturbated—and I engorged and sighed and flowed as I never had before. The beginning, although I told myself before entering a restless sleep that I never wanted to see that man again. I totally misunderstood. I genuinely thought I wanted the ice rather than the heat.

* * * *

Having made a complete fool of myself on Saturday night, I spent Sunday getting over my hangover, going to the gym, and dropping into the office and having another look at the plans for Milson Park. I left a message on the architect's answering machine, asking if he could call me to arrange a site meeting as soon as possible.

On Monday I seriously got stuck into organizing the first stage of the project. And I worked on the ones I was still finishing off on. I got back from lunch to find the architect had called, and someone had checked my diary and made an appointment already for the site meeting at Milson Park. I frowned, a bit annoyed, but I could make it so I left it.

On Wednesday I walked up to the site and looked over it yet again as I waited.

"Hi, are you Sandhurst Cullen?" a voice asked from behind me. I hadn't heard a car pull up, and I spun around, jerked out of my reverie. And yes, I had recognized the voice too, it was him. Hank, Frank whoever. Shit.

"I thought your name was Randy," Hank said angrily.

"No. Sandy," I replied in shock, "And you are Hanrob Moore? The architect?" I replied, hoping it wasn't true.

"Yes," he replied grimly.

We looked at each other for a few minutes, knowing that we had to work together.

"Um, they are great plans," I said. "Um, I'm sorry about the other night. I misheard what you said," I added.

Hank seemed to relax a fraction. I didn't; I just wanted to reach out and take hold of him. And I could hardly stop myself. I'd have fucked him right there on the bare ground of the muddy site if I could have.

* * * *

I was panicked when I fully understood it was him. I had never wanted to see him again. Or, so I had convinced myself that I never wanted to see him again. I could feel the heat starting to rise. Little did I know that it was the ice of my former life that was melting away—that forever now it would be heat, that whenever I was alone with Sandy for the rest of our lives, he would find me only in gym shorts, staving off the heat. He was that hot for me, the burning poker buried deep inside me.

I was sure he could feel the heat coming off me—that he could tell I was hyperventilating behind the calm exterior I was trying so hard to project—as he stood there and spoke enthusiastically of this Milson Park project. It was from that moment that I began to love him—not just to lust after him, but to love him for far more than what was swinging between his legs.

The Milson Park project was a small jewel, possibly the best opportunity to show creativity and both form and function that I had ever had—and perhaps ever would have. But it was a small project, something nearly every builder and architect would pass over for something big and flashy. And Sandy was talking about it just as I felt about it. He could see what I thought only I would be able to see.

He had me off balance. Quite literally, as it turned out. As we walked into the silent, deserted center of the project, I stumbled and fell into some planking. I think it made much more noise than harm, although it did stun me for a moment.

When I was able to focus again, there was Sandy. His face was close to mine, giving me a concerned look that had much more depth of feeling and interest in it than the accident warranted. And he had both of his arms around me, ready to help me up. But he didn't help me up. His lips were on mine and his body was pressed to mine there on the soft ground, amid the scattered planking.

I heard the roaring in my ears, the roaring I had heard mingled with the surf back in that convertible on the overlook above the sea during that disastrous blind date so very long ago. And I heard the sound of Ned's moans and groans from the backseat of the car as he moved between the legs of his date. But were those Ned's sounds or Sandy's sounds? Or maybe mine? It was all just too new and too strange and too wonderfully frightening to know what was happening.

It was hot, so damn hot. I was struggling to loosen my clothes. I had to escape the heat. And Sandy was helping me free myself.

The roaring in my ears. He was murmuring questions at me, and, in my panic at the newness of this, the glorious threat of this, I was whispering "no" to each of his questions, knowing that he had to stop. This wasn't what I did. This wasn't the icy me. I was so, so hot.

He had his hand on me again, but now there was no trouser fabric between his hot, hot hand and my manhood. Someone was moaning and groaning and whispering "no" to each of Sandy's questions.

He asked me if this was new to me, and, misunderstanding him, I whispered "no."

He asked me—repeatedly—if he should stop, and, misunderstanding him, I whispered "no."

He asked me if he was hurting me when his battering ram was at the gate, and, misunderstanding him, I cried out "no." And then, as he stormed the gate, he asked me again if he was hurting me and whether he should stop, and, misunderstanding him, I clenched my teeth and cried out "No! God, NO!"

And the heat flooded in, melting the iciness that had long clutched at my heart, and the hot poker split me asunder and moved inside me and filled me and stretched me.

We were beyond misunderstandings and "no." Heat and understanding and acceptance and love flooded inside me as Sandy fucked me relentlessly, flooding me again and again, driving the ice floes away with the lava of his love.

But, loud praises for the scorching release of misunderstandings—and fuck the cake; let it burn too.

Matryoshka Kidnapping

Harry Bolton had been in Beirut about a year. He was one of the more noticeable gems in the motley collection of expatriates from this or that Western country who centered our lives on the American University of Beirut for a taste of the cultures we otherwise, and for different reasons, were escaping. He was an academic from a rather vague, but obviously wealthy, American background and was a very good-looking blond. Lean and supple, clean and fresh, he looked like a retired model in whatever he wore. In winter, loose cuffed corduroys and casual shirts, with a simple cashmere jacket. In summer, well, whatever he wore, he looked good in. The package was topped off by a full head of golden blond hair and youthful blue eyes. I was vaguely aware via rumors why he was here, but all I cared was that he was here.

We had met several times, but he always seemed so sophisticated and aloof that I was afraid to approach him. And when he had spoken to me, I had lost my voice. I ached for him, but could do nothing about it but confide my passion for him to

Arnold, a British importer tucked away here more or less in hiding from several European governments.

"Him?" Arnold said, "Gee, you like a hard life. From what I have heard, he already has a harem of well-built young Arab and Turkic guys at the university who he can take his pick from."

That certainly depressed me. I was a bit old to go to university—both Arnold and I were—but we both came from established businesses that required little of our attention—his in dealings in Turkish artifacts, not always aboveboard, and I with my small regional airline. We had time on our hands and the university had proven to be a great place to pick up younger men. Arnold had tried to make clear, however, that he was here to pick me up, not some fresh, young tail. For some reason he fancied me beyond all reason. And I might have been interested, but he was an unshakable top, and, since I'd come to Lebanon, I was insisting on being the same.

I wasn't young anymore, but I was still pretty presentable—certainly Arnold, who nagged me incessantly to let him bed me, seemed to think so. I'd been to university in my native Australia quite a few years before. Like, fifteen. A long time ago, really, but I had been a serious bodybuilder in my younger days and still stacked up OK.

I'd signed up for Bolton's class on purpose, just to watch him up close—and Arnold had signed up on a never-ending quest to get into my pants. I'd known Harry was some sort of lecturer here, and his regular talks on ancient civilizations at the local museum were the reason I had originally met him. Oh, and once I had met him at a party. A museum cocktail fundraiser. He had been doing a good job of being polite and attentive and casting his smile and baby blues on the serious donors and supporters, and I had looked on and wondered how much I'd have to donate to get him to look at me that attentively.

"I hear he has a thing for Mediterranean types," Arnold added, with a sniff. "He's spent some time there on various archaeological digs and doing research and goes on about the men. Dark hair, muscular. Especially Turkic men. Hum." He grunted, looking me up and down. "When it comes to dark sultry looks, that's you, I suppose," he added. "But I thought you didn't like blonds?" Arnold was doing what he could to put me off the fetish I was forming for Bolton.

"There are exceptions," I replied huffily.

But yes, I had dark hair and was muscular, I thought, feeling as if there might be some hope after all. But Harry had hardly even looked at me when we had met. I sighed and told Arnold my attributes certainly hadn't made any difference so far. Arnold smiled happily at that.

The next week I dragged Arnold along to a lecture on the ruins of Mycenae. Harry was giving it, of course. He was looking very casual, and his blond hair was longer than usual, so it occasionally fell down over one eye. It looked incredibly sexy as he brushed it back with his long, muscular hands, and he looked incredibly smooth and hot. And I had it on good authority that his tool was a match for those hands.

We had arrived early and got middle seats in the second row, and I ogled Harry, while at the same time trying to keep Arnold's hand out of my lap. I sighed repeatedly and was aching for Harry as much as ever. I was nervously thinking about going up and asking an intelligent question at the end of the lecture, when I saw a dark, young Lebanese hunk move in on him, and the two were talking in animated gestures down at the podium. I sighed forlornly.

Arnold looked at me and rolled his eyes, "I think it's time you got over your crush, mate—or took drastic steps." I had to agree.

Some people, well most people, think I am very quiet and wouldn't hurt a fly, but Arnold knows me a bit better than that. When I am roused, I can be quite a different person.

We got ready to leave, but Arnold was dithering, and I suddenly realized that two young Turkish guys in the row behind us were talking in low voices and that the topic was sex. Well, Arnold could always listen to that sort of gossip, which I assumed explained his hesitation, and I couldn't do anything but listen too.

"Not a bad talk. Last night he fucked two of his students, I heard," one of the young Turks said.

"I heard three," his companion replied. "And that he was the one being fucked, and he wanted it rough."

"Yes, I've heard he likes taking it a bit rough. Has some fantasy about being fucked by an Australian footballer and his mates in the courtyard of an ancient villa on a remote Mediterranean island. That time I was at that party? Well he had some huge hunk of a Turk plowing him up on the back of the sofa with everyone watching. Hot. Great body for a guy his age."

"Hm." The other replied. "Yes, a great body for his age." Then they got up and left.

I was stunned. Arnold looked at me and said, "Any ideas?" and the wheels in my head were busily turning, and I was feeling roused. Yes, roughly was definitely the way I could do it to Harry.

I looked down at the lecture podium just in time to see Harry and the young stud leave by a side entrance. The young guy already had a possessive hand on Harry's well-rounded butt.

* * * *

Nabil wanted to leave right after I'd given the lecture. He was anxious to get me bedded, and I was just as anxious for him to be doing a repeat of the plowing he had given me the previous night. But I held him there in conversation. I needed to be sure that my two young Turkish friends would do what I asked and that Arnold and Howard would conveniently overhear them.

I was desperate. Beirut had been like everywhere else I'd tried. The pickings of young men had been great, but there always had been their families. And before long, I was being threatened and harassed by very well-placed families for debauching their young men. Beirut had proved to be even more threatening than most. Not only had I received death threats for having introduced Nabil and others among the cream of Lebanese manhood to my sexual preferences, but I had been hauled into what passed as an Islamic court, charged with attacking the virtue of Lebanon's young men with threats of nasty punishment to come, and now had also had my passport pulled. It was time to move on, but I was trapped—the morals police were closing in but I couldn't leave the country.

Then I learned of Arnold, the importer, and met Howard, whose family owned the airline. Howard was quite attractive and he seemed to have a good sense of humor and to be intelligent. And he was dark and handsome and well-muscled, all attributes I melted to. I easily could have happily seduced him. And in my own way and to my own purposes, I was working on that. I saw the possibility that he and Arnold could be my salvation, but I don't know if they would have helped me without what I was trying to maneuver them into. They had to live with these powerful families in Lebanon. Helping me would be a tremendous risk for them. What I've done is possibly the only way I could make this work for me.

I would love to go with Howard; I know he wants me. But I must make him want me so badly that he will accept the risks—that he will think he is the one setting everything in motion.

I broke through my internal analysis of my precarious position to find that Nabil had guided me up a side corridor and into a small storage room filled haphazardly with wooden boxes.

"I haven't much time, Nabil," I said. "If we are going to fuck, we need to go straight to your flat."

"That isn't safe anymore," Nabil said. He was already breathing heavily and had me pushed up against a wooden crate and was fiddling with my belt buckle and pulling my trousers down. "They will be watching both my flat and your house, I'm sure. Besides I can't wait. I must have you now."

And he did have me right there and then. Once we were both shed of our trousers and he was pushing his pelvis into mine and showing me how desperately he needed to be inside me, I just sighed with surrender to my own aching need and opened my legs to him. He sat me up on the rough wood of a crate top and forced his dick deep inside my passage and plowed me to cries of desire and fulfillment. I responded wildly, not knowing if this would be my last taking by Nabil—or by any man if I couldn't figure out a way to escape the prison walls that were closing in on me.

Nabil was fucking me roughly. He wasn't giving me time to adjust. And I hated this dark, smelly room and these hard, rough crates. I was all silk sheets and soft beds and pleasant music and sweet smells. Nabil was rooting like a pig, taking me hard and with ugly guttural sounds. But I hadn't given Nabil favor just because he was a beautiful young man with a monster cock. I had selected him because he was Arnold's wife's nephew.

* * * *

Harry answered his door in bare feet, wearing flimsy running shorts that showed he had great legs, lightly covered with fine gold threads of hair. On top he had on a university T-shirt framing a flat belly and good arms.

I'd called ahead, telling him I had a small carved head broken from a statue, which I had recently inherited. It was supposed to be ancient Roman, and I had said I wanted someone to have a look at. I wanted to know if it was genuine, and I'd told him that he was the expert the museum had recommended. Now I was there, he smiled, and said, "Good to met you, Howard," as if he meant it and then asked me to come in, and I followed him along the rug-covered hallway. As he walked, I watched his hard, nice, round butt cheeks flexing and moving hypnotically under the flimsy fabric of the shorts.

Grrrrrrrrrrrrrrr, I thought, let me at them, and my dick lurched. But I tried to ignore it.

After we had walked a short way down the passage, I suddenly knocked Harry forward, and he went down. He hit the floor hard, winded and shocked, and I planted my foot heavily in the center of his back, stopping him from rising however hard he struggled. Then I reached over him with my other hand and flipped the Oriental rug we had been walking over, across him. Before he could think of what to do, I was rolling him over and wrapping him up inside the rug, his arms pinned to his sides and his legs trapped.

He yelped helplessly, the noise muffled almost completely by the rug as I manhandled him, lifting him up and then throwing him over my shoulder. The rolled carpet bounced and rocked uncomfortably, and I could feel him moving and twisting about inside it. And there were some more strange noises coming from inside too. Coughing sounds. I went out of the front door and closed it behind me, then took a few steps

82

and with a heavy thump dumped the rug containing Harry onto the hard metal tray of the van I had driven up to his house in. I took the rope I had brought and tied it around the rolled rug to stop it unrolling. Good, I thought, as I tied it off. Nice and secure.

We had a long journey ahead. Arnold and a small band of Turks, including the two students who had sat behind us the other day and talked about Harry and who I had enlisted in this little adventure with the promise of a great deal of money, were waiting for me in the van outside Harry's house.

* * * *

And so it begins, I thought resolutely, as I tried my best to breathe within my dusty carpet cocoon. It had been a wild plan, with almost no chance of working. But it had started as planned. A miracle. But I could use a less dusty-clogged miracle. I couldn't breathe, and the dust in the rug was invading my throat, causing me to sneeze and wheeze. But I couldn't cough. I couldn't let Howard and whoever was helping him—Arnold, I hoped, as he was the one with the connections to that island I've heard of that would be a perfect place for me—I couldn't let my captors—no, my liberators—be stopped by the authorities.

I only hoped that they have taken the bait and the suggestions I've thrown their way and the sketchy planning I could do in the little time that had been available to me. If I were to be freed by the frenzied Howard only to find that I was still in Lebanon, I didn't know what I'd do. This time I had every reason to fear for my life. I saw the look on the faces of those four judges at my arraignment. I was just lucky they hadn't thrown me deep into their prison there and then.

* * * *

I thanked the captain for the unscheduled flight and, together, Arnold and I pulled the rolled-up rug containing Harry out of the cabin of the executive jet and slid it into the back of a small farm truck. Our Turkish helpers had gone ahead to open up Arnold's villa on this small island off the coast of Turkey that he used for his less savory import operations.

"Will Harry be OK?" I asked Arnold, indicating the small battered truck. "This thing doesn't look like it has any suspension."

Arnold just laughed at me. "Hey, you have kidnapped an American academic, rolled him in a rug, and flown him here. Now you are worried if he gets bruised? If this idea of yours is as mad as it sounds, you have a lot more to worry about than that when your Harry gets out of that rug," he responded and went off to his motorbike laughing.

I climbed into the truck's battered cab, and the weather-beaten old man behind the wheel held his hand out. I put the two fifty pound notes I had promised Arnold I'd give his estate caretaker in it. "You are a thief," I told the old man. He smiled a toothless grin, understanding the language of the pound notes but nothing that I said in English. I don't know why, but the old man's noncomprehension sent a chill up my back. Lust for Harry had made me run headlong into this wild scheme. All I could see was the chance to take him out of his element and fuck him. It hit me now, though, that I also was out of my element here. I wasn't much freer than Harry was.

"Drive," I said, waving him on, "And try to keep the ride smooth," I added. "We have delicate cargo."

The old man just laughed, put the truck into gear, and bounced down the road away from the airstrip.

The first part of the journey was fairly smooth, but then we reached the village. Once we had entered its narrow winding streets, the road improved briefly, but then the final section was little more than an old, unevenly cobbled alleyway, and the whole truck shook and bounced constantly. I was panicking, but the old man ignored my shouts telling him to stop, and all I could do was to hope that Harry was well enough padded by the expensively thick oriental rug he was inside not to be seriously hurt.

We finally arrived at the walled entrance courtyard to the old villa, and Arnold was standing there, smiling at us and holding the heavy wooden double doors open. I slid out of the cab, my legs shaking, and hurried to the back of the truck.

With the help of a couple of the Turks, I lifted the rug with Harry in it from the back of the truck and carried him inside through the heavy wooden doors that Arnold was holding open. They closed with a thud, and I imagined Harry feeling slightly frightened inside the carpet. But then I lay him down again.

The young Turks had made themselves some food while they waited for us and were now laughing and drinking coffee and Ouzo. The courtyard was full of masculine laughter, and deep pleasant voices talking. For the first time the looks they sent my way seemed a bit ominous and threatening, but I tried to suppress any feelings of uncertainty that were trying to rise within me. I had done all of this to have Harry here and helpless and mine. I had to focus on the prize.

I undid the cords holding the carpet rolled up around Harry and rolled him over, and over, unwinding the rug.

* * * *

When the carpet was unrolled and I was freed after that long, painful journey, I lay there stiff and blinking for a minute; then I saw Howard standing over me, and I also saw several dark-haired, olive-skinned, and muscular Turks sitting about and smiling down at me. Looking further, beyond the circle of men, I saw that I was in the courtyard of an old house and that the oriental rug I was lying on had been rolled out on a small paved area at its center.

I started to laugh and cough at the same time. Laughing because this was exactly what I had asked Nabil and the Turkish students to implant in Howard and Arnold's ears and minds— the description of a wild escape plan that I hoped would inflame Howard and make him set into motion my undocumented escape from Lebanon, using his airline and Arnold's Turkish connections. And it had worked. And all I'd have to do now was to let Howard fuck me, which was something I'd wanted to happen anyway. And then, with luck, Arnold would let me hide out on this island of his until I could figure out where else in the world I could go to feed my habit of seducing young men from prominent families and getting away with it.

* * * *

Harry was laughing and coughing. The coughing obviously was the result of being wrapped in the rug; the laughter must be a touch of hysteria at being completely at a loss about what was happening to him and why. But I hadn't done all of this just to give him an adventure. I ached for him. And I was going to take him now, whether or not he was willing. And he was confused and in a weakened state now, so I had best get to it. Then pay off the Turks and ask Arnold to leave Harry and me here until I could bend Harry to my will—until he only wanted me.

I bent down and kissed Harry as I stripped off his clothes and tossed them to one of the Turks, who neatly folded them and set them on the ground beside his chair. I stripped off my own clothes and did the same with them. I wanted to have Harry for myself, without these grinning Turks looking on—but I had waited too long. I had to have him now for the first time, while he was still somewhat dazed. The tenderness and seduction could come later, after I'd paid off the Turks and they and Arnold had left.

I knelt down and wrapped one hand behind Harry's head and lifted it to me, kissing him as my other hand moved down his body. My strong fingers were stroking over him, running over his flat hard belly and down, caressing and circling and squeezing his penis and balls, his tool already stiffening as he moaned in anticipation. Harry pushed out his chest, lifting himself up with his arms, as my lips moved down to his nipples. And he was whimpering too—as below, one of my fingers slipped into his entrance and he began to fuck himself on it gently. His hips worked instinctively and little cries came from his mouth as I teased and tugged his nipples with my teeth, before returning my mouth to his, losing myself in the taste and surrender of him.

I heard no signal; I did not see the shift in the circle of men around me. I was lost in foreplay with Harry, who wasn't resisting me, to my great delight and wonderment. Thus, I was completely defenseless when Arnold and a couple of the Turks approached me with the ropes I'd untied from the carpet encasing Harry and bound my hands, wrapping the rope around the base of an olive tree in the center of the courtyard so that I was leashed there like a dog.

I railed at Arnold as he stood over me and started to strip. I looked over and the Turks were stripping off their clothes as well. They had already taken their belts and trussed up Harry on top of the carpet spread out on the stones of the courtyard. Each Turk, a big grin on his face, was neatly folding his own clothes and piling them where I had placed Harry's and mine. When they were naked, they sat about the courtyard, stroking themselves up and laughing and drinking the last of their coffee and sipping Ouzo and eating as they talked in snickering tones with each other and watched Arnold begin to have his way with me. I had held him off for months, which apparently had only inflamed him more. When Arnold was well into fucking me, I saw the Turks rise, almost as one, and circle around Harry briefly before his writhing body disappeared under theirs and I heard the sounds of a lustful group taking.

Arnold was crouched on my chest, lubricating my entrance and making me whimper as he removed his fingers, two of them, from deep inside me. I moaned as he placed the head of his cock at my entrance, and I cried out to him in mixed anger, fear, and passion as he entered me. I arched my back, trying to take him as comfortably as possible, and, because he was mastering me in ways I had no idea I could respond to, I started moving my hips in rhythm with his riding of me. When he bottomed, I was moaning in pleasure and begging him to go harder. To fill me deep. He fucked me hard and deep in release of months of frustration to have at me in this way, and I came in a wild shudder and spouting of cream up his belly before he filled me with his own cream.

I should have stopped to examine my forebodings back at the air strip, when we were loading Harry into the truck. But, no, it had been too late then. I had been blind. What had been my plan to kidnap and debauch Harry had actually been Arnold's plan to kidnap and debauch me.

* * * *

The Turkish men were sitting in a circle around us, laughing and jesting with each other, their hardening cocks flopping back and forth, as I lay there on the carpet, trussed up with the belts from their trousers, and watched Arnold begin to fuck Howard. They were just sitting there, looking now at Arnold and Howard and now at me, licking their lips. Building up to something and drinking from their small cups of strong Turkish coffee and their side glasses of Ouzo. My legs were held close together by the belts, as were my wrists by other belts.

I shuddered in anticipation, though, as the Turks rose as if in unison when they'd seen Arnold bury his cock inside Howard, and they moved to encircle me. And then they were all touching me and gliding their hands on my body and becoming more and more intimate in their touch and bold in their invasions. They released my wrists and legs, but I was trapped inside their circle of writhing bodies. They had only released me to stretch me out, to open me up to their assault. There were lips and cocks everywhere. Invading my mouth and my ass, sometimes not one at a time. I was being devoured by young, well-muscled dark-bodied luscious Turkish hunks.

I loved it. It was fulfilling a fantasy of mine. It was worth the trip and all of the doublecrossing. I should have felt betrayed. I had planned for these men, precisely these men— Howard, Arnold, and my students to bring me to this place. But I thought there was only Howard to pay for that with sex. I didn't feel betrayed, however, because they were fulfilling my fetish; they were all giving me what I couldn't get enough of. I couldn't help but laughing; this whole scheme had been a deception within a deception.

At length, the Turks left me and went back to their coffee and Ouzo and light bantering. The cream of four men was oozing out of my ass, along my closely held thighs, and down my chin and chest.

I looked over at Howard and Arnold. Arnold had finished with Howard, and Howard was just lying there, trembling, completely exhausted from having been topped for the first time in many years. Arnold looked over at me and grinned. I recognized that look. A man who wasn't finished yet.

He rose and took three strides toward me and was sitting astride my hips and entering my Turk-lubricated and slackened ass with his cock. I cried out against the renewed invasion and then I cried out at the renewed pleasure of it all, as the cream of four men lubricated Arnold's frenzied pumping action, I cried for him to go deeper and deeper. All the time the Turkish men were sitting in a circle around us, sipping on their coffee and Ouzo and laughing and jesting. I had no doubt they were not finished with their own lust.

But I no longer can be sure who is in control here. Who is the master and who is the slave. Who is fucking and who is being fucked. It's all so convoluted. Just like one of those nesting Russian dolls, those Matryoshka dolls—one within another within another. All sense of order only a lie as another doll is revealed, or, in this case, as another doublecross unfolds.

And then, just as I had surmised, Arnold was off me. One second he was plowing me deep and yelping his mastery of me and the next he was gone—But only because one of the Turks, in regenerated heat, pulled him away from me and had him stretched out beside me on the carpet, on his back, his legs wide. And first the attacking Turk, turning on his own conspirator, had his mouth at Arnold's hole and then his cock inside Arnold's passage.

Another Turk was at me again now. He was kissing my mouth deeply, and I could taste the mix of aniseed and strong coffee in his mouth. I normally don't like the taste of aniseed, but the mixture of that with the coffee flavor and the essence of the Turk aroused me, and I started bucking against the Turk's cock, pulling him farther and farther inside me.

I could hear Arnold moaning beside me, being taken by a second Turk, just as another Turk also has appeared in my vision, pushed his thighs under my chest and has his cock in my mouth while the first Turk filled my ass with his rod and was pumping slowly. Thoroughly ready for this, I reached down and took the root of the young student's cock between my fingers and followed it inside my hole, opening myself wider for him. He had a hand around my cock, stroking me hard. I turned toward Arnold beside me, no longer fighting the invading Turks; lying back now and enjoying the debauching. I released the

Turk's cock from my mouth, and turned closer to Arnold and we kissed deeply and listened to the pleased chatter of the Turks all around us. I went rigid and my kissing became frantic as I ejected my seed. The intensity caused Arnold to come as well to the delight of the Turks, who continued doing a round-robin exchange of dicks in our holes.

* * * *

Hours later, Harry and I, now locked in a dimly lit, windowless room off the courtyard, were waiting our turns once more, as we listened to the sounds of the Turks gangbanging Arnold once more in his own courtyard. I turned to Harry to apologize for setting all of this in motion.

Harry just gave out a low laugh, though. "God, Howard, my brains have gotten so fucked today that I can't be sure now who set this in motion. It just looks like, with all of the confusion of who is kidnapping and fucking who, most of us have gotten what we want."

"Most of us?" I asked warily, as I rose and moved over to the door and placed my ear to the wood. I could still hear Arnold grunting and groaning out there—and the Turks laughing.

"Yes," Harry answered. "I got out of Lebanon without needing a passport or being intercepted by the morals police— and I got a fantasy gangbang by a thundering horde of luscious Turks. And Arnold got you. There's only one thing missing."

"What," I asked absently, my ear still straining to hear sounds of the gang fuck, wondering how soon they would come for me again.

"What's missing is that you were interrupted in what you wanted to do with me, what you fell into all this planning to do. But we can remedy that. Turn around."

I did so, and I made out, in the dimness of the room, raised and spread legs, strong beefy thighs covered with downy blond hair—open wide to me.

Two Chances

My car came to a stop below the front of the house, and I just sat there. It had been a long day and I was tired and not ready for the chaos I would find inside. Instead, I sat there in the car and lay my head back on the headrest and closed my eyes for five minutes of peace.

A year ago I would have been hurrying inside, however hard my day had been. But a year ago Nick would have been there, already home or on his way. Now my house, our dream house, sometimes seemed more like a burden than a place to escape the worries of the world. Four dogs and both halves of the mortgage had a lot to do with it, but mostly it was the loss of Nick. The man I had shared my life with.

I sighed and forced myself to get out of the car. Unloading the shopping from the trunk and opening the gate, I climbed the steep path to the back door. The dogs exploded to greet me, and I wondered briefly why I hadn't come straight up.

Basically because I was tired and the next day was more of the same.

I dumped the shopping in the kitchen next to the fridge and filled a glass with water and drank it as I looked about. The last time I had been well fucked had been on the kitchen bench, over twelve months before. Me wrapping my legs around Nick's waist as he pumped his thick cock up my ass in long deep strokes and I moaned and urged him on, harder and deeper. Even thinking about it now, after everything that had happened since, made my dick twitch. And if I hadn't been so tired, I might have done something about it; but then again if I remembered Nick and his fucking too well, I usually started to remember the rest.

Things happen. Nick had been working on some big advertising program that took him to Sri Lanka a couple of times close together. Then he began talking about open relationships, we started using condoms, and he went back to deal with some "unfinished business." And in between I was left with keeping the business we had gone into together going on my own.

A week later he called me from Colombo, and after an emotional conversation, I said no, he wasn't moving his new friend into our house. And eight years of being as good as married, which I had thought was perfect, was over.

I went and cried on Andrew's shoulder, and he reminded me of the clauses he had added to our business agreement, though I hadn't thought they were necessary, and the other agreement he had drawn up for us when Nick and I had built the dream house together. I had said all that mattered was that I was shattered and Nick didn't love me any more.

Two months later, when Nick had managed to get him into the country, I had been introduced to Sardi and was told I wasn't needed any more and that Sardi was taking over training Cute as Nails staff from me. I had been shocked totally but also able to say to Nick, "Hold on. You can't sack me, this is my business as well as yours." He had been fuming, but his lawyer must have been happy with what Andrew had added. Nick had to buy me out or I was a business partner with a guaranteed job for ever. And Cute as Nails had taken off. We had franchises in all major East Coast cities now. Cute as Nails was too good for Nick to walk away from, but it was still new and too hard to borrow the money to buy each other out, as I found out. Now I had an idea Nick hoped I would eventually walk away from it.

So there we were, stuck. Sardi pouted, and I had as little to do with the two of them as was possible in the circumstances.

Sardi, I had discovered when we met, was twenty, had big round black eyes the size of saucers and eyelashes so thick and long a drag queen would kill for them. Add that to perfect deep-golden skin, a lithe but muscular body, and a way of moving his ass that invited exploration, and I could see what Nick liked about him.

I wasn't bad, but I was thirty-two, looked like I worked twelve hour days, and Nick had explored my ass so often I figured it didn't hold any surprises for him any more. But I doubted Sardi would be any good at training Cute as Nails staff; for one thing he didn't like dogs.

Nick handled the advertising and signing up of franchisees, as well as still keeping in with the advertising agency he had been working for when we had first met. Nowadays he seemed to spend most of his time having coffee and driving around in his BMW with Sardi beside him. Meanwhile, I had both halves of the house, and the four dogs he used to call his kids but had happily left behind for an apartment in town and Sardi.

Nick was a natural salesman. Our business would not have existed without him, I knew. He was worth his share.

As I was putting the shopping away and fending off excited pets, the phone rang.

"Dinner," Andrew said, "This Friday, at my place. OK? 7.30."

"OK," I replied, too tired to chat.

The call was unexpected, and I wondered what the occasion was.

Andrew was my friend from long ago. He was a solicitor and a good one. Nick had never really taken to him and certainly didn't like him now. That business of the small additions Andrew had added to the complicated business agreement we had both signed when we started franchising Cute as Nails, the dog clipping, dying, and styling center that also painted their nails, had seen to that.

I arrived late for dinner, hardly surprising after the day I had had, and a quick trip home to feed the four "kids" there and change.

I made my apologies and felt a bit out of place. I was the twelfth guest, and the others, including Andrew and his partner, George, were smartly dressed and all looked fresh. I still had some dog hair in my crotch that was itching, and I had thrown on something casual. I had assumed it would be the small private dinner we sometimes had together, just the three of us. Occasionally another couple or Andrew's sister.

But it wasn't. On one side I was sitting next to a guy who looked like a male model, and I discovered had been one, but had given it up. I had no idea why. Maybe the hours didn't suit him. On the other was another guy, an American, who looked like he could have been a male model, but apparently hadn't been. The hours hadn't suited him, he said. He had a sense of humor. He said "gotten" a lot.

Hum. I tried not to scratch my crotch. I wished I had stayed at home. I went to the bathroom and dropped my pants and briefs and got a wash cloth and rubbed and washed my crotch. As I was in the middle of scrubbing, the bathroom door banged me and someone stuck his head in.

"I'll be out soon," I told him, embarrassed.

"Sorry," the American said, as I pushed the door closed.

It was not my night. I took a deep breath and hoped I had at least got rid of the itching hair. Then I dried myself and did my best to improve my appearance in the bathroom mirror. There was some improvement, and the itch seemed to have gone, and, fortunately I wasn't there to impress anyone.

I returned to the table and tried to make intelligent small talk with a bunch of merchant bankers and lawyers. They talked a lot of business talk, and I didn't mind, because I was tired and the food and wine were very good, and it was nice to be able to eat someone else's cooking and relax over it for a change. But when I tried to stand up at the end of the evening, I found I was woozy. Not drunk, but definitely not sober either. I knew I shouldn't be driving, and as there was no way I could afford to lose my license, I asked Andrew to call me a taxi.

But he spoke to Brad, the American, "Can you drop Tim off? He's on your way." Andrew said.

"Sure," replied Brad.

And in a few minutes we were off. I went to sleep in Brad's hotel car it was so comfortable, and before I knew it Brad was squeezing my thigh to wake me up. We were nearly there and he needed directions.

I apologized for going to sleep, and he said, "Don't worry about it. You look cute sleeping. I wouldn't have wakened you, but I'm afraid the hotel car driver has gotten lost."

I thought "Oh no." But his hand sat on my thigh, and I was warm and relaxed and it was having an effect.

"Coffee?" I mumbled when we arrived.

"Sure," he said and hopped out and stood up close behind me, his hands around me and resting on my belly as I tried to find the key to open the front door. Then one hand slipped down, and as I finally found the key, he had my cock cupped in his hand through my pants. And his was hard and pressing at my ass.

I had closed the front door before he was undoing my pants. I had never liked casual sex, but after twelve months, a good dinner, too much wine, and the feel of his erection pressed against me, I was unzipping him too and pulling out what he had on offer, which was quite something to behold. I dropped to my knees and began running my tongue and lips over his cap and his stiffening length, stroking the veins, licking his balls, and then swallowing him and gulping on his size as he fucked into my mouth.

Then he pulled me up and we were kissing and I was ready and wanting. I kicked off my pants and briefs, and he pushed me into the living room, and my butt landed on the high table behind the sofa. Linking a hand behind his neck, I leaned back, and he helped me lift my legs and spread my thighs wide, digging my heels into the table. His hand emerged with a sachet of lube and a condom, and I stroked his cock with my other hand as he took the lube and fingered it to my ass.

I watched his fingers slip into me. First one, my ass tight and resisting for a moment; then two, two thick fingers turning inside me, stroking. I was immediately grunting and dripping. It had been a long time, and he had a great body and a great cock and a model's face as well as those fingers sending me wild. Then we were kissing and I was yelping as he added another finger and twisted and spread them inside me. I was already moaning, my ass hungry for his long piece. He released my mouth and removed his fingers, and I guided his big cap to my rim and stroked it over myself, I came up my belly just watching. He had pushed up my T-shirt and was pinching my nipples, making me shiver as I guided his cock, and he fed himself inside me.

It had been a long time since I had watched something disappear inside my hole, and my channel knew it. I whimpered with pain as he dug deeper, not giving me enough time to adjust. But I didn't want him to stop, and I was pushing my ass to him, hungry for him to fill me. He bottomed, and I felt I'd split but wanted it all. I gasped and lifted my head for a kiss, holding him inside. He pulled out slowly and I moaned and tried to pull him back in. But when he started to pump me I cried out and lay back and pulled my legs back and widened myself.

The pumping had me moaning and arching, but it finished too quickly. If it had lasted half the night, though, it still would have finished too quickly. Brad filled the condom inside me and then fell on me and we kissed again. And then he took me again, this time more slowly and tenderly.

The wine was suddenly wearing off, and I was wondering what this guy I didn't know and had nothing in common with, who could have been a male model, was doing fucking me. I couldn't deny I had enjoyed it, but now I was dead tired and groaned at the thought that I had to drive 400 kilometers the next day to train some new franchisee.

I sat up and kissed him again, grateful for the great fuck. I doubted it was any more for him than some recompense for giving me a lift home. Within ten minutes of coming inside me the second time, he was gone. I'd forgotten all about the coffee I had offered him.

Twenty minutes later I was out like a light and dead to the world.

On Sunday I answered the phone to an American voice and it took a minute for me to realize who it was. I was embarrassed. I apologized. He asked me what I was up to, said he was horny, asked if I wanted to get together, his hotel or my place. If I hadn't been dead on my feet, I might have said yes. If he had stayed for coffee after, maybe I'd have said yes. If he'd stayed and fucked me all night, I'd definitely have said yes.

"Um. Brad, sorry, no. I'm dead . busy week. And, the other night, that's not me. It was great, it's been a long time. But I have loads to do and . . . sorry."

"Maybe some other time then," he replied, not sounding particularly disappointed.

"Yes, maybe. Thanks for the invite," I said, and hung up.

Right away part of me regretted saying no. But I had never been one for casual sex. I needed some sort of relationship. I needed talk and other stuff. Nick and I had had that for a long time, and I didn't want to settle for less. I wasn't ready to yet, anyway. Maybe in a couple more years I would be glad for any offer. But not yet.

* * * *

I wasn't sure whether I had gotten it wrong or if Andrew had said it wrong, but I had gone to his dinner party that Friday because he'd said that Nick's "significant other" would be there without Nick. Andrew was the Sydney lawyer for the American firm my dad owned, and he had fallen all over himself to see that I was entertained while I was "down under" on business. I'd fucked him in my hotel room after welcome drinks the first night I'd arrived, and that was nice enough, but I was always on the lookout for fresh meat—and these Aussie studs gave me a rush. I'd let Andrew know I'd be happy to meet any of his friends with a nice bod and tight ass and that funny accent Aussie men had.

Andrew told me there would be a male model who did some work for his clients at the party who I might fancy. Then he said he'd also invited Nick Holiday's erstwhile squeeze to the party because he was having difficulty adjusting to their breakup. Nick had been my conquest on the second night after I'd gotten to Sydney. I'd met him at a club, the Arq in Taylor Square, that Andrew had recommended. When I'd gotten my driver to give Nick a lift the morning after I'd plowed him all night, I'd met Nick's boyfriend, the luscious Sri Lankan, Sardi, at one of their dog grooming shops and had gotten the idea I'd definitely want to fuck him if he hadn't already been taken. And now he apparently was no longer taken, and I was in heat and intended to fuck someone that night. So, I accepted Andrew's invitation and assumed I'd be able to hook up with this Sardi guy at his house.

But then, everyone had gotten to the dinner party who was coming—all of the places at the table were filled—and there was no Sardi. And there I was with a raging hard on already that I needed to relieve. The Australian model—although it turned out he no longer was a model—was OK looking. In fact Andrew said that he and I made a great looking pair—but he didn't have much between his ears, which was borne out by the vacant stare he carried through dinner—I'd always thought it didn't take many brains to be a model, and here I was being offered a guy who didn't even have enough brains to be a model. And when I had gotten a feel in passing before we got to the table, it seemed he didn't have much between the legs either. The prospects for the night weren't looking good at all.

The last guy to arrive seemed a little flustered and sad and withdrawn, although he looked well turned out to me. He was the only one at the party who hadn't gotten himself dressed up like a monkey, and the casual clothes looked good on him. I was surprised when Andrew signaled to me when he was introducing us that this was the former boyfriend of Nick he was telling me about, because he certainly didn't look Sri Lankan to me. I was left thinking that Nick went through a lot of boyfriends.

The guy left the table before the rest of us were finished. He'd been real quiet during the meal, and I assumed he was just another of those dumb ones, like the former male model. I began planning my getaway so I could return to the Arq and pick up a lay for the night. I excused myself from the table to take a piss before I'd make a graceful escape. The door to the john was almost closed, but not quite. I just pushed it open, and the door was banging against this shy guy, Nick's former boyfriend, who Andrew had introduced to me as Tim.

He had gotten a wash cloth from somewhere and was dabbing at his crotch, and he had a really nice dong hanging out. This guy suddenly was looking a lot better to me. It would take me a while to get set up with someone from the Arc, and my balls were aching for a quick fuck. I decided to hang around for a bit in case I could maneuver myself between this dude's legs and save myself a trip to the club.

Andrew must have gotten a read on my mind, because when the party was breaking up, he said Tim had gotten a little tipsy and would I mind giving him a lift back to his house, which was on the way to my hotel. My mind was screaming "Bingo," as I bundled him into the hotel car and had him give the driver directions.

This Tim was a real innocent, and I lusted after him the whole trip back to his place. Once we were under way, he just leaned his head back in the seat and went to sleep. I had visions of taking him hard right there, but I decided not to give the hotel driver a show. When we had gotten close to the area where he lived, I had to squeeze him on his thigh to wake him up to provide specific directions. His thigh was nice and firm. I wanted to fuck him right then. But he seemed so sweet and distracted that I doubted I'd get the good ride I'd get out of some cruising dude I picked up at the club. I'd have the driver wait. I'd just do a quick plowing and then maybe hit the club for a better prospect for a wild night.

Tim apologized to me for going to sleep, and I decided to take the direct route, to let him know what I wanted. "Don't worry about it," I said. "You look cute sleeping. I wouldn't have wakened you, but I'm afraid the hotel car driver has gotten lost." And I kept my hand there on his thigh.

The look he gave me started off as a panicked expression, but then he sighed and his eyes went calm.

"Coffee?" he mumbled when we arrived.

"Sure," I answered. I told the hotel driver just to wait. That was fine with him. He was being paid by the hour, I'd given him a big tip already, and waiting was less hassle than taking short drives from the hotel all night.

But I wasn't going to be all night at this. This was going to be a quickie. I let Tim know exactly what I wanted and expected as he fumbled around finding his key and with getting the door open. I stood up close behind him with an arm around him and one of my palms resting on his belly. And as he finally found the key, I had gotten his cock cupped in my hand through his pants. I pressed up close behind him and let him feel the urgency between my legs. I was horse hung and wanted him to know that.

We fumbled letting our cocks free just inside the door against the wall, and I forced him to his knees and my cock into his mouth. He gave good head and had gotten me hard in no time as I fucked his mouth. Just a quick fuck and then to the club and forget this dude.

I pulled him up and we were kissing. I could tell he wanted me now. He was giving me little moans and was whimpering like he had been in heat just like I was. I figured he was still mooning over that Nick guy. But I had fucked that Nick, and I had a better cock for this guy than Nick had. Just a quick fuck and I'd leave him whimpering my name instead of Nick's.

He kicked off his pants and briefs, and I pushed him into the living room and down onto a high table behind the sofa. He linked a hand behind my neck, and he lifted his legs with my help, spreading his thighs wide. I retrieved the lube and a condom—I always come prepared—and he stroked my cock as I lubed him. And then I gave him the fingers-in-the-ass treatment. During that we were kissing and he was yelping at my fingering, giving me more pleasure than I had thought I'd get from this fuck. I extracted my fingers and brought the head of my cock to his hole. He was fully into the fuck now. He took my cock himself and stroked it over and around his rim. And then he held it and guided it as I fed my cock into him.

He whimpered with pain as I dug deeper, but he clung to me and told me not to stop. He was writhing like a virgin under me. He had a tight hole, but he was responding to me like I was the greatest lover he'd ever had. He no longer was shy and withdrawn. He was crying for me and making wild, passionate love to my cock as we fucked. This was no one-night stand. I had gotten lost in the coupling, feeling a connection I'd never felt before. Getting satisfaction from the fuck like I'd never had before.

I was spent and started to withdraw, but he held me inside him and made love to me with his hands until I was ready to ride him again. The second fuck was slower, more loving. He was quietly crying, and I found myself on the verge of tears as well. I had never felt this way before when I was fucking. I had no idea why he was having this effect on me.

When we had both come a second time, he got shy and withdrawn again. He sat up and we kissed and I could tell he wanted me to leave.

I no longer wanted to leave. I wanted to stay all night and make repeated love to him. But I could tell that the moment, for him, had passed. He didn't even mention that cup of coffee he had offered me. There was nothing else to do. I left and just told the driver to take me back to the hotel. There would be no fuck I could pick up at the club that would affect me the way this one did. I don't know what had gotten into me. I was the prince of one-night stands. "Fuck 'em and leave 'em" had been my mantra. I always left them crying for more.

But not this time. This time I think I may have fallen in love. Back at the hotel, I showered and went directly to bed—and dreamed of Tim all the night through.

I sat by the phone in the hotel room all day Saturday. Waiting for him to call. They always called. They always wanted more of me. On Sunday I ditched my pride and called Tim. I told him I was horny and wanted to fuck him again. That obviously wasn't the right approach, because he said no, that he had a busy week, no time. He said he didn't know what had gotten into him Friday night. That he wasn't just a quick lay. He didn't want me to think he did that sort of thing really. Maybe another time . . . I recognized this was a brushoff. I'd used it a million times myself. I'd just never had gotten it used on me before.

I put the telephone down gently and just sat and stared at the closed curtains at the hotel suite window. I had gotten rejected. I had finally found something I might be able to stick with, and I wasn't wanted.

* * * *

Early in the week Nick called and wanted me to catch up with him, so we met over coffee in Cremorne. Near one of the franchisees I was checking up on.

We had a half-hearted discussion about the opportunities Nick was looking at for starting Cute as Nails up in Hong Kong. I wondered why he had wanted to meet, that was more his area than mine and we could have discussed it on the phone.

"You know I miss you Tim," Nick said suddenly, and he pressed his leg against mine under the table. "You know we were always good together," he said smiling that "I wanna sink my cock in you" smile he had that made my knees go weak.

I did a double take, really caught by surprise and my cock definitely lurched.

"How about we head back to the house," he added, now running a hand up my thigh.

If we had been somewhere private, I would have dropped my pants and lain across the table so he could sink his big cock into me, right there and then. But we weren't. We were in a small café a good hour's drive from what was now my house.

I was quivering and ready, Brad's fucking may not have been long, but it had been spectacular—it had definitely turned my sex drive back on. And Nick with his Greek good looks, his easy manner and big smile had always been instant arousal for me.

"What about your apartment?" I asked, my hand under the table pulling his to my engorging dick, to let him know just how he was making me feel, and knowing his apartment was only fifteen minutes away.

"Um, it was always special in the house," he replied, smiling, but I caught the familiar twitch of his lips that told me he was not happy with my suggestion.

And that twitch was enough to make my mind cautious. "It's an hour's drive, and I am ready now," I said, in a low husky voice, "And I haven't finished the inspection here." I was still willing but wary now.

"You know the apartment's out, Tim," he said dismissively, "But I really miss you."

"Oh, so is Sardi home?" I asked pulling back.

Nick shrugged. "I miss you," he said, pouting. "Look, Sardi is, well he's not got your brains or your sense of humor Tim. You and I could always take. Sardi never has an opinion on anything. I miss you, I want to see if we can get things back on track again. You and me."

I was sitting there, suddenly melting and trembling, his hand on my engorging dick under the table, my mind thinking, "Yes take me." And I was about to say it, when I caught a movement outside and glanced up.

It was Sardi. And in a moment he swung through the café door, carrying a couple of large designer shop bags, and stopped behind Nick. Sardi leaned up against him and ran a hand possessively down his chest from behind.

"Hello, Tim," Sardi said, smiling and slitting his eyes. "I have done my shopping, Nick, much faster than I thought."

Nick didn't brush him off. Instead, his hand jumped off my dick as if it had been burned and landed on Sardi's, squeezing it reassuringly. At least Nick had the decency to look embarrassed.

"Hello, Sardi," I said politely, shaking now with anger, as well as unsatisfied lust. "I'll leave you two alone. I have to get back to the salon," I said. "Let me know how the Hong Kong business pans out." I added to Nick, smiling a fixed, forced smile at both of them.

Bastard, bastard, bastard. I thought, and I was in a rage as I left the café, and I spent some time sitting in the car getting over it before I could go back into the salon and finish my inspection.

Nick, I decided, was a complete bastard, and I had no idea how I had been so fooled by him for eight years. Now I wished I had said yes to Brad on Sunday, as that might have stopped me from getting aroused so easily by Nick.

* * * *

I sat in that hotel room and thought about Tim for two solid days. I should be angry with him. I should think of all of the inadequacies in him that I had discovered in the short time

103

we'd been in contact—or all of the ones I could imagine and manufacture. I had never, never gotten rejected before.

But I wanted him. And the longer I thought about it, the more I decided that it wasn't because he was an unfinished conquest that I wanted him. It was because I was attracted to him and he was so sweet and so vulnerable—and, yes, such a good fuck.

But I had never gotten in this position before. I'd never pursued; I'd always been pursued. And I'd rarely been the one who wanted a second coupling, who melted at the thought of doing over and over again with that same person. But I felt that way about Tim. I just couldn't help myself. I felt that way about Tim.

I called Andrew and found out all I could about Tim. I understood now why he had gotten so sad and withdrawn. I understood that he had been in a long-term relationship with this Nick guy and that Nick had moved on to the Sri Lankan and had just pushed Tim out of his life. And I heard that he was trying to push Tim out of their shared business too. So, it was understandable that Tim had gotten so distraught.

I couldn't fathom why Nick would do this. The Sri Lankan seemed like a feckless tart to me. And Tim seemed such a fine person—as beautiful in spirit as in body. I had little idea how to do it, but I mustn't let his offhand rejection be the last of it. I knew in my heart that he was worth fighting for. All I needed was a second chance. I wanted Tim—and I wanted to help him fight to keep his business.

Andrew had told me where all of the Cute as Nails shops were. I'd have gone up and down the East Coast if I had to in order to find him and beg for that second chance. So, off I went in the hotel car, having the driver stop only long enough for me to buy two dozen long-stem roses. Corny, I knew. But I was head over heels for him, had never been that way before, and had no idea what else to do.

I found him at the second shop I stopped in.

"Oh, you . . . ," Tim said in surprise as I walked up to the door, buried behind the red roses.

"Tim, I can't just . . . I . . . I've gotten . . . here, these are for you. Can we just start all over again from the beginning and give it another go?"

I had no idea what to say next, but I looked up and saw that radiant smile of his and his eyes begin to water, and I knew—or at least strongly hoped—that I wouldn't have to say anything for a while. Maybe, just maybe, I'd get that second chance.

Hookup Games

I'd been sitting reading, with the lights out and just a lamp on in the sunroom at the rear of the house. Nero heard you first, lifting his head and then going to the back door and looking about, alert. There was a full moon, and I couldn't see anything in the backyard. But I knew there was someone there, outside in the garden or the neighbor's garden. Nero is never wrong. Anna's sons go outside to make calls on their mobiles, and Nero always knows they are there before I hear their voices begin strange, one-sided, half-grunted conversations in the darkness.

But no voice started up this time. Nero stayed alert but was turned to the side of the house away from Anna's, and I felt a rush of adrenalin surge through me. Like raw heat. And putting my book aside silently, I stood and crept back into the house and to the big dining room window that looked onto the narrow side strip of ferns and hanging baskets that screened me from my neighbors.

And there you were. My pulse raced now because in the light of the full moon, I recognized the silver light reflected from the steel studs on your leather jacket.

I felt my cock jumping, and my hand reached involuntarily for it as I slipped, panting, into the deeper shadows of the room.

Now that I am totally attuned to your arrival, I hear you outside. You are trying to enter the house stealthily. I remember you from the bar the other night, and from two nights before that. You looked at me broodingly, and I knew you wanted to hook up then, but I wanted to run you; I wanted you to want me so badly you'd track me down and take me roughly.

You were rough trade; that's why I was attracted to you at the bar. Just what I want.

I know it won't take you long to find the back door open and break into the house. I rush back there and grab Nero and carry him to the spare room. I drop him in there and close the door, hoping he understands that tonight I don't want a guard dog to protect me.

Then I hurry to my bed, and I hear a creak on the back step as I strip my clothes off, tossing them aside in a frenzy to be naked, so I can arrange my body in a provocative pose that I know will arouse you. I spread my legs for you, pretending that I'm still asleep. I want you to enter me thinking that I'm still asleep, that you are taking me unaware, roughly—against my will, supposedly. But, of course, not really.

I want it rough, and I want you to think you are taking it from me. I'll fight you, but only briefly. I'll let you overwhelm me. I want you to think I have melted to you, almost against my will. I want you as long and thick and virile as possible. I want you moving deep inside me, roughly and fully taking me.

* * * *

I had seen you in the bar several times and watched men swarming around you like bees around a honey pot. And I had seen how you loved that open attention, and I looked away as I was not one to give you that or to compete. But when I looked back, I found your eyes fixed on mine, and I knew I wanted you more than any of them did.

Then last night I sat closer, waiting for an opening, and you laughed, as someone felt you up with his mouth buried in your neck, adding loudly, looking my way, into my eyes, "I like it rough sometimes. I like to be surprised. Overcome."

Soon after, your groper and his friend had pulled you up and you had left, arms wrapped about each other. And I had followed the three of you, my body aching to have you. I zipped up my studded leather jacket and climbed on my bike, imagining you between my thighs, curling my body over my machine and for once regretting the deep throbbing rumbling roar it makes as I move off, following the white Saab you three are leaving in.

I stay back, hard to do when I want to roar up to the Saab and drag you from the car and from your smooth friends. Then throw you down on your back before me on my bike and drive into you, your legs kicking wildly as you struggle, before I show you the paradise my hard-driving cock can give you, your legs then embracing my hips as I ride you.

Tonight, though, I am creeping around your house under a full moon, wondering if I am mad. I am a weekend warrior, the leather and bike toys allowing me to play at being something I am not, wanting to be as different when I cruise the male bars as I can be from my "real" life. But I am big and muscular, and I look dangerous. And tonight I want you to believe I am, as I find the open back door, and the step creaks, and I climb inside your house.

Silence. I stand frozen, listening. Then suddenly a voice is talking somewhere, and for a moment, I panic. Then I realize it is someone outside, away from the back door, talking into a phone. I breathe rapidly, the adrenalin pumping and my cock pressing against my jeans. I am even more aroused now by what I am doing.

You are on your bed, tossing and turning, restless, and not knowing why, tangled in the sheets when I find you. And you don't realize I am there, so I watch you for a while moving in your half sleep, your cock half full and your hand lying on your belly, resting in the curly hair that runs down to your bush. Your legs are spread, and one is slightly bent, and I am stroking myself into full hardness, overcome by lust for you and wanting to take you as you wake, take you suddenly and powerfully as if I am a stranger and have overcome you in some fantasy. Possessing you completely, entering you roughly, making you cry out repeatedly and spill your seed between us, before you realize who I am.

I strip off quietly outside your door, never taking my eyes from you, seeing that you are having a nighttime arousal and your cock is growing as I watch.

Naked, I enter your bedroom, and my meat is rock hard for you. I strip off your sheet and in the same motion am kneeling between your thighs as I grasp your legs and push them wide. You are suddenly awake and struggling, but I am too strong for you and force you down. One hand covering your mouth to stop your shouts, as my fingers dig roughly for your hole. My body pressing you back, stopping you escaping from me.

You grunt and struggle, but I have now got possession of you, my fingers buried inside you, feeling your heat and smoothness. Your organ is a rod pressed to my belly as mine lies throbbing against your thigh. Three fingers are probing you now, and you shudder and spout cream up your belly. Yes, yes. I slide my cock and belly against you, feeling its creamy wetness.

Now you are struggling less, and I have your legs wide and my cock head is searching for your entrance and finds it.

Yes. I am rough and brutal as I enter you. Force gets my nob past your rim, as you buck your hips trying to throw me off. Then I am in, buried in your sweet channel, and my arms, gripping you in a bear hug, I lift you up and keep you immovable as I roll my hips and work myself inside you.

I am lost in a dream and the smell of you and the sound of your moans and my grunting.

"Oh baby," I murmur as my mouth searches for yours. "Baby, baby."

We kiss. Mouths possessing and arousing. You move with me, and I ease my tight hug so that you hang back slightly, away from me, and I watch your face as you run your hands over your body and mine, stroke yourself, and moan to my fucking. And you can see now who I am.

As you ejaculate and spill your seed between us, I come deep inside you, my semen flowing into you and possessing your center.

Later, as we lie there, you curled against me as I lie around you, my tumescent cock resting inside you; I confess to you that really I am an accountant. You sigh, kiss my hand, lying under your head, and say, "I knew that."

Turtle Airways

Turtle Airways departs daily from Madai $20 to Castaway, the note read.

I'd found the piece of yellow paper, torn off something larger, sitting on the dresser of the hotel room when I came out of the shower. I turned it over. There was no indication who had written it or left it there. But the lack of punctuation meant it definitely wasn't Roger.

Well, I thought, why not? I had quickly seen most of what the small island of Madai had to offer, and Roger, well, hum . . .

We had come away for a holiday, making noises about relaxation, sun, and days filled with sex. I had been ready. More than ready to be fucked long and hard. And the first night Roger had obliged me, though after a sleepless night, an early morning, and ten hours of flying, the sex had been more a great release— that had seen us both asleep within an hour of hitting the bed. But when I awoke in the morning I was hard and thought there was plenty of time as I rolled over. To find that Roger was already gone.

* * * *

This was a last-chance effort for both David and me. And I had assumed it would end badly when he booked us for Madai Island, which, if the brochures were to be believed, was perhaps the dullest place on earth. David no doubt thought that this would cause me to focus completely on him and reach some sort of revelation that he was the only man on earth for me. Fat chance of that, though.

David had known my lifestyle when we first hooked up. We were opposites and that initially had excited us both. David, the shy but meltingly handsome maturing man, successful in business and staid as they came—until I got him into the sack, and then a volcano of lust underneath me, pulling me deep inside him and crying out in passion and writhing under me. And I, the young party boy, easy to know by anyone who wanted a supercock grinding inside them, loud and always ready for action.

I had let David convince me to move in with him, and that was our big mistake. As long as we could keep our encounters to equal turfs, separate lives, our fuckings were like a match touching a can of gasoline. But once I was in David's house, in his bed, inside his life, he slowly but surely tried to change me to his lifestyle, his temperament, his "safe on the surface" and "constant to one another" ways. And the match was fizzling out.

I had tried to tell him this a million times. I was happy the way I was, and, yes, I loved to fuck him, but I didn't want to be him. I was casual; I loved the risk of the hunt. The height of the fuck, the ejaculation, no matter the hole it was in, was the "all" for me. His talk of love and caring and commitment was just getting too old and was coming between us, creating an ever-widening chasm. I was not ready for commitment, and he was oh so smug about declaring that there had been no one other than me from our first fucking.

That was fine for him, if that was what turned him on. But it wasn't fine for me. And bringing me to an isolated, dull island wasn't going to change that if I had anything to do about it.

When we arrived at the hotel after a long, tiring flight, David ordered a meal in the room. I wanted to at least take a walk around the area the hotel was in, with some hope of seeing where there might be action. But David said no, that he wanted to eat in, then fuck, and then sleep the sleep of the dead. And the next day he wanted to go golfing. It was obvious that he wanted us to focus entirely on each other in this vacation—that he was concentrating on pulling me into his world and holding me close to him. Even when I'd seen a nice little piece of ass in the hotel lobby, someone apparently connected with the hotel, because I first saw him walking out from behind the reception desk—and the sweet twink had given me an extra look and a big smile—David had latched on to my elbow and pushed me toward the stairs to the rooms on the upper floor.

The obvious moves to control and isolate me made me grumpy, and I let that bubble out during our dinner, eaten on the balcony overlooking the sea. It didn't help to be able to see people out on the beach, having fun, in the waning hour of sunlight, when it was just David and me on a closed balcony, crowding each other for space. I was feeling stifled.

I intended to snub David, but, pushing the dinner trays aside, he sank to the floor of the balcony and unzipped my shorts and started working my cock with his sweet mouth. He was such an expert at the suck, and I was so horny—all of the time—that he won. Shortly thereafter, I had him prone across the bed on his belly, and moved to a position that drove him wild with lust and thus sent me to the heights of desire, as well.

I started out crouched over him, my pelvis between his stretched legs and fucking hard into him from the rear, with my hands pushing down on his shoulder blades. And then, when I'd gotten a good rhythm going and he was panting hard and crying out for me, I started revolving around on my cock buried deep inside him, testing his channel walls at every angle, until we were feet to head and I was grasping his ankles with my fists and pounding my meat down into his canal at a reverse angle that drove him wild. This was the David that I liked, the "let it all loose" David, pounding his fists into the bedspread, biting into one of my calves, his chest heaving with the exertion, speaking dirty to me of wanting more and harder. This was the David who didn't care that it was me and only me churning around inside him, the David who was transported by the fuck itself—reaching the height of personal pleasure that was my goal in life.

I had exhausted him so well that David was dead to the world and snoring quietly when I arose again, early in the still-dark morning hours, pulled on a tight T and my jeans, and silently left the room. The sex had been good. But the isolation was smothering. I needed to get out of there and get some action—or at least find some personal space. And maybe a little danger.

I went down to the hotel's bar, which was deserted—all except for the sweet twink I had gotten a rise from when I winked at him in the lobby upon our arrive. He was behind the bar, cleaning glasses and taking inventory of the liquor, getting set up for the next day.

We engaged in a little bit of innocuous chat as we shared a glass of scotch. But I hadn't misjudged the nice piece of ass's response to my signaling earlier in the day. He came around the bar and sucked me off as I leaned against a barstool. And then I fucked him hard on top of the bar, his butt on the polished black glass surface and his legs held wide for me, while I knelt between his legs on the bar stool and pumped him three ways from Sunday.

This was what I meant. Casual, joyous action. The risk of discovery by anyone passing by the bar and looking in. Taking the opportunities when they came. Putting myself in positions to get plenty of opportunities. No commitment, no angsting about the feelings of the other. Offering what I knew was an extra long, thick cock, and delivering it to any attractive man who wanted it. And this hotel barkeep obviously wanted it, as he squealed his delight of how I stretched him and reached deep inside him and jerked the cries of lust out of him.

After I was done, I asked him whether there was any real action to be had here. He regretfully said that there was little on Madai itself, but that if I wanted to hook up with a guy with a talented channel who was always ready to go, I should take a day trip over to another island, Castaway. Once there, I should go down to the west beach and ask for Tony. I told him that sounded interesting, and he took up a yellowing receipt pad from behind the bar, wrote down instructions for me, tore off the fragment he had written on, and handed it to me. It read, *Turtle Airways departs daily from Madai $20 to Castaway.*

Turtle Airways, I thought. Only David would bring me to a remote island whose airline was called Turtle Airways. That was David all over; wanting to pull himself and me into a shell. I returned to the room to get my Speedo, snorkel, and fins. I didn't bother to wake David. I just could make the first daily flight to Castaway if I hurried, and I wasn't in the mood for an argument with David over acting on impulse and seeking adventure.

* * * *

At the airstrip I wondered for a moment if I should have left some sort of message to let Roger know where I had gone. But no, I thought for the tenth time, I was sick of him running off, and I doubted he'd even notice I'd been away.

It was a small plane, Turtle Airways was a very small operation. And as I was crawling in and squeezing myself onto a narrow seat beside the female half of an oversized retired American couple, I briefly had second thoughts.

The other passengers were two young couples. The boys hardly men yet, and still not filled out, and I had seen them throw a bag full of snorkels and flippers into the luggage bay. The girls with them were young and fluid, still lean hipped and slightly immature. One sat up next to the pilot, flirting with him, and the other three sat in the backseat against the rear wall of the cabin, the second girl giggling and wriggling between the two whispering and laughing boys.

The American woman set her lips in a thin line and looked back at them disapprovingly. I was only going for the day, I reminded myself. And maybe Roger would notice I was gone. Or maybe not. I had no one to blame for that but myself. I had said yes to an open relationship when everything inside me had screamed no, knowing how much Roger liked to party—and I had set no boundaries on how open the relationship would be.

Castaway came up below us as a crescent-shaped green jewel, rimmed with pale gold and set in a crystal clear blue ocean. The plane banked sharply, and we landed on the lagoon in a short bumpy flurry of spray before settling into the water and pulling over to a couple of natives in crisp white resort uniforms, who were waiting on the pontoon at the end of a long, narrow jetty.

I clambered out and stretched, breathing the clean fresh salty air in deeply. Then I was handed my small bag by the pilot and trailed off after the young people with our snorkeling guide leading the way. That was what we had come to do, snorkel. It wasn't something I was mad on but to get to Castaway you had to have a booking of some sort, and snorkeling had been all that was available apart from accommodation, which I didn't need. I gathered the elderly couple had come to stay—lucky them, I thought. The beauty and quiet of Castaway was more to my taste than busy Madai.

Our guide took us along the beach to a thatched cabana, and there I was equipped and joined the rest of the party already waiting to head off. The four young people were making their way, yelling and laughing, into the water before I even had my snorkel fitted.

"They're a happy bunch," I said, envying them their relaxed casualness and youth.

"Hungh," the guide snorted, "They will scare everything away. They are here for fun, maybe sex, not to see the fish, or the coral," he replied, giving me a flash of white teeth. "If you want the fish, we will have to go over to the left away from them. That is where I'll take the rest of you," he said

When I was ready, he led us into the water and toward the left.

I was still getting used to the snorkel when something brushed my calf and I flipped in the water, scared for a moment that a shark was after me. Before we set off we'd been warned about a dozen fatal things we could encounter in the lagoon.

But it was another snorkeler who was behind me, a faceless man with a golden muscular body and black hair waving in the ocean. I turned away and swam on, trying to work out which one of our party he was, but knew I didn't recognize him. No one on the beach had been a bronze god. I swam on, following the rest of my group, swimming over an uneven bottom that was now scattered with coral outcrops, where small colorful fish occasionally flitted in and out.

The god kept nearby, but behind me. I slowed down, but he stayed back still. I stopped and turned to him, but he swam by me, not even seeming to look at me. So I resumed, following the tour group, and in a moment he was there again, hanging back just behind me. I suddenly had the idea that maybe he hadn't paid for the tour and was hanging back, trying to stay out of sight of the guide and had no interest in me as anything but a screen.

Ah well, I thought, at thirty-eight that was understandable; I was fit but had never been a bronzed god, even when I was young.

We had reached deeper water now, and large rocky shelves, and outcrops moved silently beneath me as we swam on. The touch on my calf came again, then he took hold of my leg, and I wondered what he was playing at. I stopped and turned and he swam in closer and gripped my waist and turned me and pulled me back against him. Then his arm was pointing down. Down into a fissure between two rocky outcrops covered in corals and anemones. Beautiful. I looked down, yes, stopping was worth it. The sea floor just there was a whole world on its own. And now that we were being still, small fish started to appear from all over, flitting in and out and pausing to nibble daintily on the corals and rocks.

He was holding me close, and I suddenly realized that that hard lump I could feel pressing against my back was his cock. I relaxed against him, and he wrapped an arm about my belly, laying his palm low and pressing in, and I almost moaned at the feel of him. But he was pointing his other arm down and moving his finger across the fissure and my eyes followed where he pointed.

I wanted to gasp when I saw what he was pointing to, but the snorkel stopped me, and I had to watch silently as it slowly emerged. It was massive. A groper perhaps, but nothing like I'd seen on TV; its size and power was nothing like I had imagined. The fish was nearly as long as me and would have weighed many times more. If it had taken a swipe at me with its tail, I knew I could be badly hurt.

I lay a hand over the one on my belly and squeezed it, telling him I could see and was amazed. He pulled me in closer, almost like a lover, and my head rested against the side of his, and my back was plastered to his front, with his hard rod caught between us, where I could feel its heat. I was glad I wore a baggy swimsuit that hid my own erection.

The groper flipped his tail and was suddenly ten meters away, eating a fish I hadn't even noticed. When it was gone, there was another tail flip, and the giant fish had turned and was gliding effortlessly back into the fissure. In a moment he had disappeared.

My companion was now cupping my basket in his free hand, and I reached back behind him and clasped his butt and was pulling him in tighter. Then I moved my head wrong and spluttered as water came down the snorkel. My companion pushed me up so my head broke the surface, and we both trod water as I spluttered and coughed and cleared my equipment. He still had his mask on and I couldn't see his face clearly.

He moved in closer and was running his hands up and down my torso, his chest brushing mine, his hard cock pressing against mine. I looked about, but there was no one watching, so I went with it. I striped off my mask and reached for his and pulled it free. I didn't recognize him, and half his face was rough—scarred by something—but his eyes were bright and clear and his mouth was smiling widely as it moved in to mine. In a moment we were locked into a kiss and our bodies were aligned in the water, moving against each other as we kept treading water to stop from going under.

"Shallower," I gasped, "I need to stand. I'm not used to treading water as . . ." I didn't say, "as I get ready to fuck," but I certainly wasn't going to be able to do both things at once.

He laughed, kissed me, and said, "Follow me." Then he pulled his mask up and mouthed his snorkel. He held my hand and tugged at my arm as he sunk down beneath the surface. I followed him, and we swam side by side back to the beach.

Within minutes we were inside a beach cabana that opened straight onto the sand, and he was stripping my sodden swimsuit off and pushing me down on to a huge bed in the center of the cabana. And me? Well, I had my legs up and wrapped them around his hips and pulled him into me as his tongue invaded my mouth. We were both wet and slick, and the breeze turned the water cool so that I was shivering and rubbing against him for warmth as the breeze dried my skin and the heat rose inside me. I wasn't into casual sex, but I knew I wanted to be fucked deep and hard by him, whoever he was. And after the experience he had shared with me on the reef, he certainly wasn't a stranger.

He stripped his own wet shorts off then, and I saw the long cock I had been feeling and was now aching for. I fell on the thick pole that grew out of his nest of black pubic hair and sucked him as well as I could, but he had other ideas and was soon pushing me back, turning me over, and pulling me up onto my knees. I moaned and writhed, wanting him inside me. Then he took lube and a condom from beside the bed, and I rested my head on my arms and widened my legs as he moved between them and began to play with my entrance. He rimmed me with lubed fingers and tongue, and my rim quivered and relaxed for him, and I was begging him to fuck me, as his fingers entered my well-used passage, stroking around its walls as his other hand reached under me looking for my throbbing tool.

In moments I was moaning and coming, and he had added another finger to my ass. I bucked back on his hand as he stroked the last drops from me. Then it was his cock that was sliding into me, and I was moaning and joining his rhythm, grunting, "Yes. Yes. Deeper. Faster."

But he plowed me in a changing rhythm for what seemed hours as I moaned and whimpered happily. The action on my prostrate had me filling again, and with the help of his hand I came for the second time, just as he came deep inside me. We fell together on the bed, my mouth seeking his and his arms winding around me.

We lay like that, spent and recovering, until a strange buzzing sound filled the room and he moved away.

"Hello," he said, and I felt foolish, realizing the buzzing had been the phone sitting beside his side of the bed.

"Ah," he said, and laughed. "Yes, I know where he is, I will get him," he said smiling and handing me the phone. "It's for you."

"For me? How did they—?"

"Your snorkel guide saw us come in here. He knows what I do in here. He does it in here too. No big deal."

I was suddenly in shock, wondering what disaster might have someone chasing me to Castaway.

"Yes?" I said into the phone.

* * * *

The Turtle Airways flight lived up to its name. It took them forever to get off the ground, and we were only up in the air for about ten minutes, and then it took them forever to pull the eight-seater up to the open-air shelter they called a terminal. But as soon as we deplaned, it was getting ready to taxi off to return to Madai for the next flight.

It didn't take me long to find the west beach. The dark-skinned island native who drove me there in an ancient Peugeot taxi seemed to know just where I wanted to go. I'd told him that I was looking for Tony at the west beach, and he drove me right to a small hut near the end of the beach and stood hanging on his door, as I walked all around the hut and confirmed that it was deserted.

"Tony doesn't seem to be here," I said as I came back around the side of the hut. "You wouldn't happen to know where he might be, would you?"

"My guess is that he's in Singapore, visiting family," the taxi driver said, and then he gave me a big, white-toothed smile.

"That's an interesting guess," I said. "Why would you guess that?"

"Maybe because I drove him to the airport yesterday," the taxi driver said. And then he grinned.

"And you didn't know this back at the airport?" I asked. Pretty snotty bastard, I thought, but I tried hard to remain polite, because he was a big, hulking, massively muscled brute. There wasn't much of a question who would win if we got into a nasty fight.

"Men coming to the island and looking for Tony mostly are looking for one thing," The big grin explained. "And are you looking for Tony for that one thing, maybe? I can do that one thing as well as Tony could."

The hut wasn't locked, and we stripped each other hurriedly in the dimness of the one room and next to the pile of woven palm-leaf matting Tony must be using as a bed. The taxi driver was big and bulging all over. A veritable native warrior built for strength and endurance.

We were struggling for dominance. I was a dedicated top and always had gone with men who I could control physically. There was no controlling this big, brown monster, though. We moved into a sixty-nine position, with each of us delighted and impressed with the cock and balls we found. But when I moved my tongue to his ass rim, starting into preparing him for entry, he did the same with me.

We wrestled for several minutes more, rolling around and off of the matting and onto the packed-sand floor, which had some give to it, as my cheek and chest and knees were pressed into the earth when he had gained dominance.

He had strong arms woven in under mine, pinning me down in a full Nelson, and I screamed out in frustration, followed by pain, and then stretching almost to the point of splitting as his cock gained purchase in my ass canal and began its long, throbbing, wriggling journey up into me. He was laughing and grunting and biting on my neck and shoulders, and I was writhing and crying out in violation and anger and helplessness as he started up a rapid pumping deep inside me.

After a while of useless struggle, I gave up and relaxed, letting him have his way with me. And, probably sensing that we had arrived at what I wanted all along, he loosened his strong grip on me and concentrated on the plumbing of his cock inside me and the pleasure it gave him. It was all a ruse on my part, however. When the hulking taxi driver thought he was home free and had fucked all of the fight out of me, I gathered my strength and reared up off the sandy floor, sending him lurching off to the side and knocking the breath out of him.

Then I scrambled up and ran for the door. He was too fleet of foot for me, though. I feinted toward the taxi, and when he committed to heading me off in that direction, I turned and ran for the water line.

He caught me in the surf and pulled me out to sea, dunking my head under the water and wringing all of the fight out of me. He crouched there, chest deep in the surf, his bulk and weight helping him to stand solidly against the breaking waves, and continued to press my head under the water, occasionally pulling my head up by my hair and giving me a few precious seconds of breath before he pushed my head under again. All of the time, he was holding me in his lap, his cock once more encased inside me and thrusting and pumping.

At the point of his ejaculation, I could hold my breath no longer, and I blacked out as, my head being held viciously below the surface of the water, I began swallowing in the salty sea water.

* * * *

"Hi," David said. He was sitting next to the hospital bed, watching for Roger to open his eyes. And, at long last, he had done so.

"Hi back," Roger answered, attempting a weak smile, which turned into a brief, hacking cough.

"God, that tastes awful. And I'm so thirsty," Roger continued after he was able to control himself.

"It was all the sea water you took in," David said. "Lucky you were quickly found washed up on the beach. A taxi driver found you. They had to pump a lot of water out of you."

David was looking so concerned that Roger took his hand and kissed it and than laid it on his chest. David smiled through his tears and moved the hand under the sheet and laid it right where Roger had put it, but now it was skin on skin. He worked Roger's nipple in distracted circular movement, not realizing he was doing so, just falling into an old familiar pattern. Roger said nothing, enjoying the feel of David's attention.

"So, do you want to talk about it?" David asked. "It was risky for you to be out there by yourself. You always take too many risks."

"Yes, I can see that pretty clearly now," Roger answered in a weak voice. "And no, I don't think I want to talk about." His wan smile shut David up. And Roger could clearly see now how much David cared for him. Maybe, he thought, maybe I can give a little. That really was too risky.

"David—"

"Don't say it," David cut him off. "I went too far on that. I know I've crowded you too much. I've tried to change you. I've treated what we have almost like a marriage. I know you didn't sign up for that. And I know I've been missing out on a lot by being too possessive and tight-assed myself. I can understand your need for a looser relationship. The attraction of that has come to me too . . . quite recently."

"Shush, it's OK, baby," Roger murmured, his hand going up to David's face to brush away a tear. "It's OK, we can—"

"Oh, God, can we give it another try, a more serious try?" David blurted out, overriding what he was afraid Roger was building up to say.

"Yes, yes, I'd like that," Roger answered, and he put a hand under the covers and guided David's hand from his chest down to his crotch, letting David feel just how ready he was to try to make a go of it. "I think we can manage, just if we both bend a little and concentrate on what we have together."

About the Authors

Shabbu is the combined pen name for two established authors, one on the East Coast of the United States and one on the East Coast of Australia, who spin erotica together in cyber space.

Habu, a bisexual former supersonic spy jet pilot, intelligence agent, and diplomat, is a published mainstream novelist and short story writer under another name and in another dimension of his life.

Sabb, once an accountant and sometime property developer, is a wild barbarian at heart, who knows that love is out there of you're lucky enough to find it.

You will find them at www.BarbarianSpy.com and an extensive offering of these authors erotic, writings are published by BarbarianSpy. All books are available from Amazon, Barnes and Noble, KOBO, Apple ibook store, All Romance Ebooks, Bookstrand, Smashwords and many others. Habu is also published by eXcessica LLC.

BarbarianSpy
FOR LITERARY HEAT

Not all books listed below may currently be on release.
* indicates the book is available in paperback and e-book.

BOOKS BY DIRK HESSIAN

Xtreme Erotica

The King's Men
Shores of Tripoli
Prophecy of Noto
Pretender's Fate

General Erotica/Romance

Fire Down the Valley*
Constantinople*
The Beautiful Way*
Blue and Gray
Colonel's Treasure
Beginning of Time
Labyrinth

BOOKS BY HABU

Gay Erotica

Memoir Faction

Flying High, Diving Deep*

Xtreme Erotica

Apyko: The Greek Pimp
Visits of the Schlange
Second Coming: Emile La Cour Unleashed
Vortex: Sacrificed by Curiosity*
Dark Angel Sounding *(in e-book & included in Sounding:Ultimate Control Paperback)**
Sounding: Ultimate Control (*Print Only*)*
Sounding Five *(in e-book & included in Sounding:Ultimate Control paperback)**

General Erotica

Romance

Snowy, Snowy Nights (Christmas Romance)

Four Coins
Lower Than the Heart
Brambleton
Gotta Keep Trying
Finding Amnad
Platres Conclave
Other Novels/Novellas
Cruising Gigolo
Prepared in Cape Verdi
Gilded Cage
House on Park
Anything for Ambition
Dance of the Ravishers
Hard Knocks U*
My Neighbor's Spa*
Man's Man: Tales of a High Priced Gay Hooker*
Trip Money
Clint Folsom Mysteries Compendium Volume 1*
Death to Blonds - Stolen Judgment (Clint Folsom
Mystery)*
Clint Folsom Mysteries Compendium Volume 2*
The Indian Doctor
Sailorboy
Home to Fire Island
Choke Hold
Gay Erotica Anthologies
Spy Tales 001*
Spy Tales 002*
Doubled*
Doubled Again*
Tails in the Tropics*
Tails in the Med*
Tails in the West*
Rough Riders*
Grab Bag 1*
Grab Bag 2*
Grab Bag 3*
Grab Bag 4*

Grab Bag 5*
Beyond the Beaded Curtain*
Habu's Christmas Balls
The Sporting Life*
Fetish Galore!*
Literary Gay Erotica
Cairo Surrender*
The Handyman*
Homeward Bound
Journey to Mirage*
Menage Erotica
Cruising Gigolo
13 Ways for Halloween
Luther*
The Indian Prince
Literary GLBT Fiction
Summer of Denial
BOOKS BY SHABBU
Finding Jason
Dirty Pool
Operation Black Jade
Cigars!*
Angel in the Barn
Gayly Complicated*
Despoiling David
The Tree of Idleness*
I Met a Man
The Interview
Rough Road to Happiness
BOOKS BY SABB
Hiring in Hollywood
The Legend of Holleystone Grange
Surprise Encounters
She is He
Wrong Man
Loyal to his King
Barbarian Tales - Book One - Traveler's Tales*
Barbarian Tales - Book Two - Journeys Begin*

Barbarian Tales - Book Three - The Inheritance*
Barbarian Tales - Book Four - Road to Persepolis*

~